Mainstream • Wom... • ... • Music Cds

Edit et Cetera Ltd.

Nonfiction • Young Adult • Children • Poetry

Presents

Ragamuffins
of the
Fifth Ward

by

Charles S. Novinskie

Florence,
I hope you
enjoy my stories
of growing up
in the Fifth Ward

Charles S Novinskie
1-29-06

Edit et Cetera Ltd., a small publishing company in Grand Junction, Colorado, is pleased to offer a line of books for readers who yearn to enjoy great stories without the explicit sex, gory violence, and obscene language that permeate so much of today's literature and entertainment. We're calling this line Family Book House. Under its umbrella reside a number of genres—women's fiction, mainstream, love stories (broader category than romance), mystery, suspense, young adult, fantasy, historical fiction, and children's books. Our stories have family themes and stress the value of family relationships. Nonfiction and selected volumes of poetry will also be offered. We hope you are as excited about this new line as we are. Please ask for our publications at your local bookstore or look for them at amazon.com. See current titles available in the back of this book.

If you have questions or comments, you may contact this author at charlie@familybookhouse.com. Or visit our website at www.FamilyBookHouse.com.

Dedicated to

*My mom, who taught me the
importance of reading*

*My kids, each of whom taught me
something different about myself*

*Kristine, my loving wife,
who taught me the truth,
and the true meaning
of love*

Ragamuffins of the Fifth Ward

Edit et Cetera Ltd.
Grand Junction, Colorado
www.FamilyBookHouse.com

First Printing: October 2004

ISBN: 0-9746122-4-3

Cover Design: Claude St. Aubin & Jaysin Brunner

INTRODUCTION

What comes to mind when you think back to the era of the sixties and seventies—Watergate, Vietnam, civil unrest, racial tension? Nah, not if it was 1968 and you were ten years old—that was the stuff adults worried about. All we had to worry about was who was stronger, The Hulk or Thor? Or how many doubles of Y. A. Tittle could one kid actually end up with before getting that Johnny Unitas card? And why, oh why, did Topps make that rectangular piece of gum in all their cards so very, very hard?

The 1960s era was dubbed the Age of Innocents, and with good reason. Children were under the protective wings of adults—spared the anxieties that our parents faced as we entered into an era of war, of high tech death and destruction. It was almost as though an invisible barrier had been erected, defining the fine line between childhood and adulthood. Breaking the barrier was a one-way trip. Once done, it was impossible to return to that childlike state that made everything as simple as night and day.

The sixties had many dark days—the United States' involvement in Vietnam, the assassination of President Kennedy, the Bay of Pigs, the cold war and the threat of a nuclear attack, the assassination of Martin Luther King, Jr.—and yet as preteens growing up in that era, we could remain oblivious to those issues. That's why we had parents; that's what adults were for, to deal with adult problems caused by adults. Not only did we not want to have an emotional attachment to these tragic events, but the adults seemed to do a great job of protecting us from the real problems of our day. I believe, as horrible as those events were, adults found solace in the fact that they were able to insulate the children from many of the horrors of that era.

Of course, a lot of fun things happened in the sixties—the exploding popularity of the Beatles, the debut of Star Trek on television, and man's real life star trek—the landing of man on the moon. Taking pleasure in the fun things and filtering out the bad things in life created the real balance in childhood. Our perception that all things bad were caused by adults was a very real attempt to prolong our own entry into adulthood.

Being entertained involved imagination and very little money—the reverse of today's form of entertainment! Comic books, pick up baseball games, trading cards, skateboards, fireflies, candy, and crew cuts all occupied our time and energies. There was a sort of naïveté of growing up then—no rules or regulations to ruin your fun (or so we thought). The sixties were a carefree, laid back time when kids could be kids and growing up was something far, far away.

Comic books were twelve cents, and they were a magical balance of words and pictures collectively known as pop art. Baseball cards were bought as much for the stick of hard, pink bubble gum as for the cards themselves. Candy was a sight to behold—sold in loose, bulk quantities, not wrapped in today's win-something-for-free gimmicky wrappers. Yep, growing up in the sixties was a kid's dream come true! Being a kid meant something—fun without being hindered by adult intrusions. We could amuse ourselves all day long without fear of getting in to trouble, or worse, something terrible happening to us.

Growing up meant that summer was king. The ringing of the school bell on the last day of school was a sound unlike any other! It was as though the bell signaled the start of a giant race that lasted the entire summer. Hot, humid, and hazy, the last day of school ushered in the start of the lazy days of summer. And the lazy days of summer were just that—lazy—but a kid never had more fun nor expended more energy doing absolutely nothing.

The fond memories of growing up in a coal town in the sixties are retold in this series of short stories of childhood in Shamokin, Pennsylvania, during that era. Granted, the town in that decade was on the cusp of an economic downturn that continues to this day. When the coal mining industry collapsed, it was as though a part of the town's soul went with it. Nonetheless, the gang of the Fifth Ward, of which I was a part, didn't understand the economic climate of our community. All we knew was that we didn't have a lot of extra money and that we didn't need a lot of expensive extras to have fun! In most cases a ball, bat, glove, and a pocket full of change were more than enough to last us for days on end.

While the stories in this book are not presented in any kind of chronological order, all of stories took place between 1963 and 1971. The first few years I lived on South Shamokin Street, hence the title, *Ragamuffins of the Fifth Ward*. Later stories take place after my family moved to Stetler Drive, located in the Edgewood section of town. All of the tales relate experiences during my first eight years of school at St. Stan's.

When I first started writing these anecdotes, I believed they were rather ordinary—common to anyone who spent his or her formative years growing up in the sixties. But after writing story after story, I realized my experiences were indeed unique, not because of their place in time, but due to a combination of where I grew up and the time period. The sights, sounds, and tastes that assaulted my senses were as different as those of the community.

At this juncture I should explain Shamokin. Some say the town was named after a great Indian chief, Nikomahs, only spelled backwards. While I can neither confirm nor deny that claim, it does seem odd that if you were going to name a town in honor of someone, you would spell the name backwards! Like many municipalities back east, Shamokin has been around a long time. Not the prettiest of towns (due mostly to the scars left behind from coal mining operations), it does embody a certain beauty that a long-time resident can appreciate. Rather than thriving on an infusion of new buildings and businesses, the community hangs on to long-established, traditional businesses that have solid family values. A quick trip through Shamokin finds many of the same stores being operated by successive generations.

Traditions handed down from generation to generation provided a strong bond among those in the community. Many of the early settlers came and stayed because of their mining skills. Several of my own Polish relatives settled in the area to work in the underground anthracite coal mines, maintaining a precarious hold on their deep-rooted traditions. "When Coal Was King" was often a battle cry of the region, reflecting a generation of hard working miners during an era when Vaudeville acts toured there before moving on to the big time. Indeed, "When Coal Was King" referred to a time period that predated the Second World War. As the coal production slowed, so did the local economy. And yet the hard working, honest people of Shamokin found a way to carry on.

Today, a cornucopia of senior citizens make up much of the population, and they're hoping for a time when an economic upturn will make its way through Northumberland County and provide jobs for the next generation of proud Shamokinites! And yet there exists a certain mystique that endears one to the community. When Friday night rolls around, it's as though the entire town shows up at Kemp Memorial Stadium for some of the hardest, smash-mouth football found anywhere east of the Mississippi. Kids cruise Independence Street as though gas were still thirty cents a gallon. And a trip down that same street is like a trip to Mayberry—the people are just as friendly, hard working, and affable as Andy Taylor and Aunt Bee. Sadly, many of the places mentioned in this book no longer exist. Ravaged by time and progress, they have faded into the sunset.

Never again will these unique rites of passage be repeated. Technological advances and changes in attitudes have supplanted the simple pleasures recounted here. Because such joys of childhood may be a thing of the past, this book has been written as a reminder of that special time, a tribute to the Age of Innocents—to growing up in the sixties.

FIRST DAY OF SCHOOL

School was never easy for me—not grade school, not high school, not college. In fact, it only seemed to get harder and harder. One thing I did manage to do was make it through at an early age. I started when I was five, graduated parochial school at thirteen, high school at seventeen, and college at twenty one. Don't get me wrong—it wasn't because of my stellar scholarly performance. Instead, it was a case of my being at the right place at the right time.

In 1963 I was enrolled in kindergarten at St. Stan's Catholic School at the tender age of five. Starting school back then was a lot scarier than it is today. Now both parents often work, and kids spend a few years in preschool, getting prepped for kindergarten. Not so in the sixties! Back then, Mom was called mom for a very good reason—rather than spend her days working an outside job, she stayed home to raise the kids while Dad was off earning the paycheck.

Going off to kindergarten was as far removed from spending the previous five years at home with Mom as I could ever imagine. The first day of school was perhaps the most traumatic event a five-year-old would ever go through. Not only did you have to make sure that your pencils were sharpened, but you also had to make sure that all of your primary colors were included in your crayon box!

For me, kindergarten was a nightmarish experience. I'm not ashamed to admit that I started to cry soon after Mom dropped me off, and not all the promises in the world that it would be okay were going to appease me. Now I'm not talking about those fake crocodile tears that all kids learn to shed until Mom or Dad is out of sight.

These tears started early in the day and didn't stop! Not even for recess! Conventional wisdom would suggest a call to Mommy. Instead, a small miracle happened that day. The layperson in charge of teaching kindergarten had no idea what to do with me, so she took me over to the first grade to have a seat while she discussed the situation with one of the nuns who was in charge of the school—and I immediately stopped crying!

Now my recollection is a bit fuzzy from that point on. I don't know whether the sisters actually forgot that I wasn't really in the first grade, or they figured that my absence of crying was a sign to leave me there. All I know is that, just after turning five, I had gone from kindergarten to the first grade!

No more morning naps, cookies and milk, and playtime for me—I was now in the first grade! Looking back, I'm pretty sure this five year-old was nowhere near ready for the rigors of first grade. Hey, if they'd understood my real reason for crying on that first day, they probably would have concluded that I wasn't even ready for kindergarten—forget about first grade! I guess it all turned out okay, but I still have this recurring dream where the police show up at my door, arrest me for fraud, and take away my college degree and high school diploma, stating the indisputable truth that I never graduated kindergarten!

THE THREE R's

Saint Stanislaus Kostka Catholic School—St. Stan's for short—was where all the Fifth Ward Catholic kids of Polish descent attended elementary school. The school, a typical red brick schoolhouse located on the hill known as Race Street, was the place where we spent our days learning the three R's—religion, religion, religion! The hallowed halls of St. Stan's taught us, our parents, and probably their parents, everything we needed to know to get by in the real world. And then there was religion, religion, religion.

We didn't really have a lot of normal people teaching in this school—well, by normal I mean laypersons. I still don't know what a layperson is—I just know that they dressed just like our parents, and they apparently weren't allowed to talk about religion. And then there were the nuns—sister's, nuns, whatever. I don't know where the moniker of nun came from, but I knew that by the end of eight grades that if I never saw a nun ever again, it would be too soon. These nuns were the toughest women I've ever met; they could make the women's section of cell block three break down in tears! Heck, just walking around in those long, black robes in the heat of summer was more than enough to toughen anyone up! I can still envision those black robes with white braided ropes for belts that tied around their waists and hung by their sides like a hangman's noose waiting for its next victim. The black habits with white brims covered their heads with never a lock of hair showing. Sister Superior was the leader of the bunch, and all we learned early on was that it was certain death to be sent to her office! We did see kids actually return from trips to the

Mother Superior's office, but they never dared speak of it!

There was a sameness to the uniforms the nuns wore, and it was even worse for us kids attending the school. A typical uniform for the boys consisted of black or blue slacks, black shoes, white shirts, and red bow ties. The girls wore white blouses, plaid skirts, and black buckle shoes. Daily inspections required the girls to kneel in front of the class to make sure their skirts reached the floor. This made for some interesting fantasies and a sure guarantee that skirts were at least knee-length.

Seating in school could make or break your entire school year. Unlike today's mobile class schedule, we never changed desks, never changed classrooms; instead, the nuns would change based on subject matter. One nun would come by for geography, one for math, one for religion, and so on.

Your desk was your domain. Each desk had a top that could be lifted up, providing the perfect place to hide the types of things you hid from the nuns of St. Stan's. It became your refuge, and you hung on to it for dear life. For me a desk in the last row along the outside window was my key to surviving the school year. Letting my mind wander as I stared out the window was a favorite pastime. My former favorite pastime was staring at the clock, counting the minutes to recess, lunch, and the end of the day…until the nun placed a sign under the clock that read, Time Will Pass, Will You?

Sure, we got a pretty solid education that included learning a lot of English, a little Polish, and a bit of Latin, with science and math thrown in. But mostly, it was religion, religion, religion. Even though one sister was assigned to teach us one religion class per day, every other nun felt it her duty to also instill her depth of religious dogma on a less than enthusiastic audience. After about ten minutes of geography, we spent the remainder of the class talking about religion, the same for math class, and science class…and so on and so on…five days a week, nine months a year.

One of the finer points of parochial school that I could have done without was the disciplinary tactics employed by the nuns. Forget everything you've ever heard about the horror stories of abuse in Catholic schools by the nuns—because it's all true! While we did learn respect for authority, I still have not-so-fond memories of rulers-on-knuckles of all the lefties in school because "it was the Devil that made you write left-handed." If you don't believe me, ask anyone who went to a parochial school in the sixties.

Being locked in dark closets and having notes pinned to your clothes to be read by your parents were just the beginnings of a normal school day. Sure, a note sent home doesn't sound like much these days, but back then the note-pinned-to-your-clothes (and not knowing what it said) has no modern day equivalent! When a note from school was seen by Mom or Dad, it meant that you did something wrong and annoyed the Sister. So you could count on additional punishment at home!

Corporal punishment was not only acceptable, it was encouraged (obviously before the days of pediatrician Dr. Spock). If you were unfortunate enough to be sent on the long trek down the hall to Sister Superior's office, you were sure to encounter the "Board of Education." Don't get me wrong, this Board wasn't a group of people, but rather a solid oak paddle with holes drilled in it (for good air flow) that was delivered directly on your bottom, not once, not twice, but usually three times. I used to think that three times thing was a scriptural requirement, but I have not yet been able to find it.

I'm not saying that corporal punishment was a bad thing. Let's face it…when you're eight years old, you sort of figure that's what the nun's job is. The funny part was that the punishment was always meted out by the nuns. Never once did I ever see the priests of the parish lay a hand on any of the kids. In fact, when I think back now, the priest always sat down and had "a chat" with you. The only thing I could figure was that the nuns had an arrangement with the priest—sort of good cop, bad cop. Whatever the reason, the outcome was the same—all of us grew up with a healthy respect for our peers, peppered with a healthy dose of the fear of authority thrown in for good measure!

THE PLAYGROUND

The word playground had a very different meaning when I was growing up. If you think of a park-like environment with swings and slides and sandboxes when you envision a playground, you'd be right. But for those of us in the Fifth Ward, the definition of playground was much more literal. Our playground was the ground on which we played. The playground we visited consisted of a three or four block radius from our houses—and what a playground it was!

To the south we had a wonderful end-of-the-road turnaround that was home to the local concrete plant. Just to the south of the cement plant was the old roundhouse that serviced and switched out train cars. Roundhouses, to the best of my knowledge, no longer exist. I haven't seen once since growing up in the Fifth Ward. For non-railroad buffs, a roundhouse was a huge, round building that served as the hub of a giant wheel, the spokes of which radiated out from the center in the form of railroad tracks. The train's engine would pull into the roundhouse, and then the roundhouse would rotate until the engine lined up with the rail cars that it was to hook up with. This was quite a sight for a bunch of kids who had aspirations of one day working the rails!

The west end of our playground consisted of Mulberry Hill, a wonderful place for a variety of activities. Many an adventure revolved around that hill.

Kolody's store was the extent of our travels to the north, and why not? Kolody's offered an assortment of gems just waiting for our nickels and dimes.

Many of the businesses in our town also served as a place of residence. Every block had at least one corner store that would allow a person to pick up necessities like bread, milk, and meat—and some items not so necessary, like comic books and trading cards.

The east end of our travels usually ended with our backyards since Shamokin Creek was the eastern boundary and not a very pleasant place to hang out.

Hanging out with the gang in our backyard
with our multi-purpose tent!

Necessity dictated that the four block radius around our houses serve as a microcosm of activity. After all, it wasn't easy loading up the Radio Flyer wagon and hauling a day's worth of toys to our playground. Yellow Tonka trucks were required for playing at the concrete plant. A variety of items including wagons, cardboard, shovels, and sleds (in the winter) were necessary for the daily conquest of Mulberry Hill. Backyard play often consisted of some sort of pitched tent that served as a fort, hideout, or tepee, depending upon the games we had in mind.

A trip to Kolody's was reserved for whenever one of us had a nickel or dime to spare on candy or trading cards—usually baseball cards!

Sure, we did have an area full of fancy playground equipment, but a kid with a great bunch of friends and an overactive imagination couldn't have imagined a better playground than the Fifth Ward!

MULBERRY HILL

There's something about a mountain that attracts kids. Maybe it's the rocky outcrops, or else it's the grassy meadows or gentle swaying of the trees in the wind. Whatever it is, a nearby mountain spells one thing—F-U-N!

For the gang at the south end of Shamokin Street, our very own private mountain was known as Mulberry Hill. Not a giant hill like those of the Rocky Mountains, it was rather a kid-friendly height that we could easily scale in a few minutes time. The greatest thing about Mulberry Hill was its provision of four seasons of fun—in the spring and fall the hill was a great place to fly kites. In the winter it provided the perfect sled run, and during the summer it offered us hours of wonderful cardboard sliding!

Cardboard sliding, I'm afraid, is a lost art. Any piece of cardboard would do, and we searched the neighborhood for discarded chunks of corrugated boxes. The bigger the piece, the more we could fit. For those of you unfamiliar with cardboard sliding, the act was as simple as gravity itself. All you needed was a sheet of cardboard, a steep hill, preferably with some nice green grass, and a warm body to add mass to the mix. Steering was impossible and hanging on was an acquired skill. If you made it half way down the hill, you considered it a successful run. A dozen or so runs down the hill and you had all the ingredients for an afternoon of inexpensive fun.

"Fun" might not accurately describe all of the runs that were made down Mulberry Hill. Scraped knees and elbows often marred an otherwise successful run. A wrong twist here or there meant deviating from the worn, prescribed course down the hill, leading to a date with disaster.

One particular day we thought we had run into the mother lode of cardboard. One of the neighbors had purchased a brand new refrigerator, complete with cardboard box—a really *big* cardboard box that could easily fit 3 or 4 of us at one time. The hardest part was hauling the box to the top of the hill. Crawling inside the box, we proceeded to slide down the hill, the box gliding over the dry grass like a hydrofoil over water. I don't think I've ever laughed harder sliding down the hill—that is, until that tranquil ride turned into a nightmare of epic proportions.

Hitting a gooney (that's a big rock in kid talk), our cardboard box rotated 90 degrees, and we were trapped inside, tumbling down the steep hill like a loaded cement truck charging down Glen Burn Mountain without brakes! Bodies bounced everywhere. We all tumbled head over shoulder as we plummeted toward the bottom of the hill. Now don't get me wrong here…in the mind of an eight-year-old, blindly rolling down a hill in a box with two of your closest friends is about as close to having fun as any of us could ever have imagined.

The real problem arose when our cardboard box came in contact with a ground hornets' nest. It's hard to describe the feeling of tumbling down a hill in a box with your friends when all of a sudden the box is full of angry, buzzing hornets. Picture three kids and a hornets' nest turning round and round in a dryer, and you begin to get the picture. We shot out of the box faster than a circus performer shot out of a cannon! The only problem was the hornets weren't as amused as we were, and they continued to sting our arms, legs, and heads. To this day I can't tell you how many times we were all stung—but I do still remember screaming and crying all the way home. I also know that we never went back for that cardboard box for fear of being attacked by more hornets.

HEAD OF THE CLASS

There was nothing quite as important in grade school as the seating arrangements. For those of us not yet old enough to develop real cliques with our fellow classmates, the seating pecking order was instrumental in keeping us out of harm's way. Anywhere in the front row assured you that you were going to end up as either teacher's pet or teacher's whipping boy. Trying to find a seat that fell under the nun's radar was crucial to surviving the school year.

The front row seat closest to the classroom door was the hot seat. No first grader in his right mind would ever willingly sit there. That seat carried way too much responsibility. Any knock at the door had to be answered by the person seated at that desk. When the priest came for a surprise visit, the person in the first seat was required to make note as the priest opened the door and would stand up, signaling that the priest was in the room. Then all of the other classmates stood and chanted (in their best drone voice), acknowledging the priest by name. To this day I have no idea why we were required to do this. All I remember is that the procedure was repeated whenever the priest left the room. It's plain to see that no one in their right mind would ever sit in the front row seat closest to the door—in fact, that spot was always taken by one of the girls in the class.

My favorite seat was in the back of the room, furthest from the front door. From that vantage point I could see everything that was going on in the classroom.

Keep in mind that, back in those days, our desk was our personal domain. We never changed classrooms, but rather spent our

18

entire day in the same room in the same seat. The school desks were as old as wood itself—long rows of desks with wrought iron sides and wooden seats that folded up. Desktops displayed numerous carvings of long-forgotten kids who had gone before—complete with the round hole known as an ink well and a long, horizontal groove that was the resting place for a number two pencil. The desks were attached in rows from front to back on long, wooden rails, which were bolted to the floor. Some of the desks had an opening compartment that was accessesed from directly under the desk tops; others had a hinged top that lifted for access into the compartment.

Desk and desk location became part of your identity in school, providing a status within the classroom. The smart kids sat up front while the class clowns and troublemakers sat near the back. Slower kids scattered throughout the room. When a new school year started, the scramble for the desk was essential.

One of the first undertakings when getting a desk was to carve your initials into it—often using the sharp end of your compass. In case you don't remember, a compass was an instrument with two legs connected at one end by a pivot. One leg had a sharp point, and the other allowed a pencil to be slipped into it. The compass was used for making perfect circles of any size. After using the sharp end of the compass to carve your initials, you then smudged the carving with your lead pencil to give it that its-been-there-forever look. Getting caught carving your name in the desk meant an immediate trip to Sister Superior's office! I don't know whether they even make compasses anymore, but I'm pretty sure they wouldn't let you carry one on an airplane today! (This is a perfect example of yesterday's tool becoming today's potential weapon.)

The advantage of being in the back of the room was that you were able to find a lot of little points of distraction. For me it was the large windows just to my left. Now when I say large windows, you have to understand that this school was the type of redbrick schoolhouse built sometime in the early 1900s. These windows stretched from just above the radiators on the floor clear up to the ceiling, which was probably twenty feet high. The panes of glass were so old that the glass had actually started to droop and sag, giving everything that you looked at outside a strange, distorted look. My favorite time of the year was late spring, near the end of the school year. It was warm enough outside to open the windows and let in all of the sights, sounds, and smells that kids crave when stuck in school. The windows hinged and pivoted in the middle—the top half of the window would swing in while the bottom half hung outside. Once the windows were opened, my mind would float right outside like a dandelion on a gentle breeze!

THE DRAWER

Did you ever dream of a place where you could find all your favorite comics and trading cards? How about your best shooter marbles or jacks? What about all your favorite candy? What if you could find all those things in one place?

I knew of such a place—Sister Ludgard's lower right hand desk drawer in the seventh grade! I have no idea how she did it; the desk drawer was a normal, everyday sort of drawer in an otherwise plain oak desk. But somehow, day after day, she managed to stuff it full of everything we held sacred! Rumor had it that tunnels ran under St. Stan's School, and I wondered whether her desk drawer was a direct access laundry-chute to those lower labyrinths! We had been told so often that comic books and trading cards and candy were the Devil's toys that I imagined her drawer having a direct link to Satan's personal furnace.

Of course, there were other times when I wondered whether the drawer lead directly to the convent where the nuns lived. I often pictured them sitting around in the evening, eating mouthfuls of candy and reading the best comics that twelve cents could buy!

I never did see the inside of that desk drawer—I just knew that whatever went in never again saw the light of day, at least with its former owner. All we knew was that we didn't want our hard earned money wasted by having our prized possessions end up there. Logic dictated that you wouldn't bring such things to school. To a kid, logic is an abstract concept! Often our recesses consisted of buying as many taboo things as we could think of in the hopes that we could get them past the nun and back out of the school at day's end.

For me it was comic books. I'd buy them four or five at a time and find a way to get them to my seat and stashed in my desk. While I got pretty good at getting the goodies into the school, I couldn't wait to get home to read the latest issues of *Spider-Man* or *The Avengers* or *Hulk* or *The Mighty Thor*. For me there was no greater feeling than getting away with reading the latest comic book during whatever classes I had in the afternoon.

One of the many classic comics produced by Marvel Comics
in the 1960s—AVENGERS #4, reintroducing
the Golden Age superhero, Captain America!

Thor was one of my favorite comics. According to Norse mythology, Thor was the god of thunder. His dad, Odin, was the ruler of all the Norse gods and pretty much omnipotent—which pretty much means being all-powerful or having unlimited authority.

One afternoon during religion class, the nun called on me because she knew I wasn't paying attention. She was going to prove to everyone that she had caught me once again! I guess she was feeling pretty omnipotent, but her downfall came when she hit me with the least expected question of all—she asked if I knew the meaning of omnipotent. Figuring I had no clue, she headed towards me when I shouted out the definition as being all-powerful and being the ultimate authority. Well, that stopped her dead in her tracks and sent her back to the front of the room, where she continued on with the lesson. The bonus for me was that I was reading a *Thor* comic stuck in the middle of my religion book and that Stan (The Man) Lee, the author, didn't talk down to kids in his comics. If you read *Thor* on a regular basis, you knew the meaning of the word omnipotent!

Reading comics in class became a real science. One of our favorite tricks was to make our own book covers out of paper bags from the grocery store. In fact, all of my books had covers made from the brown bags. When it was cut and folded just right, I could not only slip the ends of my book into the jackets, I could fit a comic between the paper cover and the front of the book. Hence, I could carry five or six of my school books with a comic hidden in each book right past the nuns, and they were oblivious to the fact. Sitting in back made it easy to slip out the comic so that it could be slipped into the middle of an open book. This may sound a bit strange, but the balance between paying attention in class and reading comics in class helped me with my reading and vocabulary in the long run.

But I'm digressing in my discussion of "the drawer." No one knows what happened to the many possessions that were collected and placed in that drawer. I would have to guess that I probably lost dozens of comics over the course of the school year. I also saw candy, gum, trading cards, toy dolls, toy trucks, paddle balls, jacks, and other cool things get sucked up into the drawer. I wonder how much money would all that stuff bring on eBay today?

A LITTLE OFF THE TOP

Ted the Barber was his name, and giving haircuts was his game. Whatever name you went with, G.I., crew cut, or buzz cut, there wasn't a lot of science to it. A pair of electric clippers set to scalp, a few quick passes, and whamo!—one *very* short haircut! Long before the modern day barber shop, i.e., the beauty salon, made its way to our corner of the world, the barber shop, complete with striped pole, ruled supreme. Hair cuts consisted of one style and one price, and I can only imagine that barber school of the 1960s consisted of a one day course made up of proper care and handling of electric clippers and instructions on plugging it in. Then move clippers in a rapid but constant motion from the front to the rear of the head. Repeat.

Haircut day was a special day, and kids lined up to get their turn in the chair. In fact, while we may not have been crazy about the haircuts, the waiting-our-turn was the best time a kid could hope for. For those of us growing up in the 1960s, the barbershop was the precursor of modern day bookstores. Or at least that was how it felt to this ten-year-old! Sure, there were the standard tools of the trade—electric clippers, scissors, a straight razor complete with a genuine leather strap for sharpening, a dusting brush, talcum powder, and the ever present glass container filled with blue-lilac liquid that was designed to sterilize the combs—but off in the corner was the mother lode of reading excitement, comic books!

Fantastic Four, Superman, Batman, Spider-Man, Sad Sack, Little Lulu and more—the table was full of comic books. Best of all, the comics were always different from the ones that had been there during my last haircut. Where they came from wasn't important; the fact that waiting your turn for a haircut allowed you time to peruse this wealth of reading material *was* important. The haircuts were always short, in length of hair as well as time taken to administer it, but the time spent drooling over that special combination of words and art was more than worth a trip to the chair.

The annoying aspect of Ted's amazing pile of comics was that all of them lacked the top halves of their covers—almost as though they had spent some time in Ted's barber chair before making it to the reading table. Every comic book was missing its title. Years later, I learned Ted's collection of comics was ill-gotten—books scheduled for destruction.

In the early days of newsstand distribution, comic books (and magazines) that didn't sell were stripped of their cover logos, which were returned by store owners for full credit. Then the books were supposed to be destroyed. However, throwing them away when they were in good condition, other than the missing cover, seemed wasteful. Enterprising store owners saw the benefit of having them resurface somewhere that kids would hang out. After all, if they got hooked on the comics, they'd come searching out new ones! And, of course, sales would increase. Now I don't know where Ted the Barber's near-coverless copies came from, but I'm sure that haircuts were much more enjoyable due to the fun found in the four color entertainment at his shop.

Barbershops are as rare today as finding comic books on the newsstand. That made me wonder whether the loss of that magical combination of haircuts and comics led to the downfall of barbershops…or perhaps even the downfall of comic books!

With the steady proliferation of fancy, upscale salons and the decline of the official, striped-poled barbershop, I long for those days when you could get a great buzz hair cut and a free read of a comic book! Not too long ago, when my wife owned one of those fancy salons, I had the opportunity to bring in comic books—with complete covers—and leave them for the kids to find. And now that buzz cuts are back in fashion, I can almost envision ten-year-olds lounging around, reading comic books while waiting for their own haircuts. Hey, I can almost smell the lilac water!

PATROL BOY—SUPER-HERO

The closest I've ever gotten to being a superhero was in the seventh grade when I was a bona fide patrol boy. Donning an orange plastic sash that crossed my chest and hooked around my waist, I was in full costume for my superhero role. It even came with a silver star, giving me an almost deputy-like authority over other kids my age.

My duty was a solemn one. I was entrusted with the safety of all my classmates. Not from some everyday mundane threat like a passing car, no, *much* more important—I was stationed at the bottom of Race Street at the intersection of Pearl Street, where the trains passed on a regular basis!

Coal mining was still a viable entity in Shamokin in the 1960s, and enough coal was produced that most of the trains coming out of the roundhouse were coal trains—long, long coal trains with dangerous loads of coal, tons and tons of coal! My alter ego of Patrol Boy made sure that none of the other school kids tried to beat the train or run under it. Sure, I'd let the kids put pennies on the tracks if the train was still a ways off, but crossing under a moving train was a definite no-no.

Penny flattening was a regular fun thing we did with spare change. Placing pennies or groups of pennies on the track, we would see just how flat a penny could get. After the train passed, we searched the ground for the still warm, paper-thin wafers of copper. Seeing the force of a passing train and the effect it had on a copper coin provided the perfect way to convince my classmates that trying to sneak under a long line of slow moving train cars was something we never wanted to do.

One reason we waited for the train to pass was because the trainman at the back (in the caboose) always greeted us with a toot of his whistle and a handful of candy. When he tossed the sweets toward us, we scrambled along the ground for the free goodies.

While we found a number of ways to amuse ourselves with a passing train, I'm happy to report that not only did I successfully complete my task of patrol boy without ever losing a classmate, but I also got out of school a full ten minutes before the final bell sounded. Looking back, I'm quite thankful that no one ever fell victim to the coal train on my "watch." The reality of it was that at least once a week, usually Tuesdays, I hopped the train and was a long way down the tracks before the final bell ever rang. The train ran right through downtown Shamokin and past Kleese's—the best place to buy comic books in all of Shamokin!

Kleese's no longer exists, but in the sixties and seventies it was the perfect place to pick up the best comics on earth! Magazines received special treatment and were racked on the higher spaces of the shelving. Comics, stacked in piles on the floor near the magazines, were at the perfect height for little tykes to skim the piles of those four color gems. The Tuesday shipments usually consisted of two or three stacks of books, with each stack about eight or ten inches high. Various books, from *Archie* to *Marvel* and *DC* were available in multiple copies. Arriving before the rest of the kids allowed me to pick the best copies available.

Not all of the comic titles made it to Kleese's, and it took careful planning to coordinate a Tuesday trip to four or five stores in order to buy copies of every title available. The real key was planning the trip so that you could hit all of the stores and still make it home in time for supper!

A CARD FOR ALL SEASONS

Most people measure seasons by the calendar. A ten-year-old with pocket change, however, measured them by the appearance of a two-and-one-half by three-and-one-half inch piece of cardboard, better known as a baseball card. Spring and fall weren't just seasons—they were special events marked by the arrival of the first packs of Topps baseball cards in the spring and football cards in the fall.

While the adults awaited the sighting of the first robin or the first early bloom breaking through the ground, the gang in the Fifth Ward eagerly anticipated the coming of the first pack of baseball cards to Kolody's corner store. One thin dime bought a wax pack of cards—complete with the ever-present stick of pink Bazooka gum.

Not many people realize this, but in the early days of sports cards, the gum was added to help sell the cards. Bazooka gum, complete with a Bazooka Joe™ comic, became an American staple shortly after the Second World War. Known as Topps Chewing Gum, Inc, the company, then based in Brooklyn, grew their gum business into a trading card empire. Because the cards weren't an overnight success, the gum was included as an incentive to buy them.

The Shorin Brothers started the Topps Company back in 1938. Selling off a chain of Brooklyn-based gas stations, the Shorin family hired a consultant to determine the next big craze—and that craze was bubble gum. Given that Topps Gum became Bazooka Bubble Gum around the time of the Second World War, many folks figured the term Bazooka was named for the shoulder-hoisted grenade launcher. It wasn't! The bazooka referred to was actually a musical

28

instrument popular during that time period!

By the 1950s Topps was producing trading cards featuring TV and movie cowboys, Hopalong Cassidy being its first major trading card success. It took a few more years before Topps hit big with the modern day baseball card—1952, in fact—the same year that Mickey Mantle and Willie Mays made the baseball scene.

Original artwork for an early Bazooka Joe™ comic strip

Topps later became famous for gross-out cards like Garbage Pail Kids and Wacky Packages…and, of course, the most sought-after card set of all time, Mars Attacks!

Collecting for us became a real passion, and we could open and trade dozens of packs of cards in a matter of minutes—all the while shoving multiple sticks of gum into our mouths! I always wondered why the pink stick of gum was so hard—even in a freshly opened pack. Years later I learned that the process involved in cutting and inserting the gum in the packs required it to have a certain stiffness!

Whereas the appearance of baseball cards marked the start of spring, football cards signaled fall's arrival. One of my favorite cards was a Y.A. Tittle football card. I'm sure Tittle was a great player in his own right, but this group of ten-year-old just thought it was cool that we could get away with saying "tittle"!

One of the greatest aspects of trading cards was the fact that there were so many doubles and triples. Opening just a few packs guaranteed your getting the same card over and over again. The great part of possessing all those doubles was that you could take three or four cards, clip them to the frame of your bike with a clothespin, and bend them in to your spokes, giving you the greatest sounding "motor" bike a sports card could buy. In fact, I was convinced that constituted the entire reason for all the double and triple repeats. I admit a small degree of disappointment when I later discovered the meaning of collation and how multiple-pack purchases of cards increased sales for the trading card companies.

BROWN BAG LUNCH

Every person experiences a moment in life that forever defines his or her very essence—that first kiss, a first car, getting beat up in school for the very first time. That event, good or bad, helps to shape one's outlook on life. For me, such an epiphany manifested itself in the form of a brown paper bag in the third grade cafeteria at St. Stanislaus Grade School!

Don't get me wrong...the food, prepared by volunteers—mostly elderly women with blue hair—wasn't that bad. In fact, on the whole, it tasted pretty good, if a bit monotonous. Thanks to advance warning in the form of cafeteria menus provided prior to actual consumption, a brown bag lunch could be more desirable than the hot, nutritious meals served cafeteria style. Most kids participated in lunch swapping. Peanut butter and jelly one day would be traded for a bologna with mustard. But on this day the trading of brown bags was prearranged, and not nearly as meaty. But I'm getting ahead of myself...

One of my favorite parts of the school week was receiving the latest order form for the Scholastic book club. Reading, even in the third grade, was very important to me. Whatever money I could scrimp and save (i.e., beg my mom for) ended up going into an order form for paperback books from Scholastic. While I had a real passion for reading, my absolute fascination was in collecting *Peanuts* paperbacks—as in Charlie Brown, Snoopy, Lucy, and Linus. Little did I know at the time that Charles Schulz would create comic strip history by producing *Peanuts* strips for half a century! Something

31

mystical about the combination of words and pictures captivated me at an early age—and has hung around for nearly 40 years.

Having said that, I'll return to my topic and the new experience looming on the horizon—well, new for me, anyway. One of my classmates, whose name I no longer remember, provided one of those defining moments that altered my life.

While I was fascinated with the *Peanuts* books provided by the Scholastic book club, I began to dabble in the world of four-color words and pictures—comic books! It started out innocently enough—a *Sad Sack* comic here and *Archie* comic there. The real appeal in the beginning, however, was that comics were taboo at St. Stan's. Just the thought of a comic book entering the hallowed halls of St. Stan's parochial school sent shivers up the sisters' habits.

And that's where the brown bag came in—the perfect cover for a bag of comic book gold covertly traded during a lunch-hour exchange! My fellow classmate had boasted about having quite a collection of comic books—mostly in retaliation for my boast of having every *Peanuts* book ever published by Scholastic. As much as I loved my cherished *Peanuts* paperbacks, I couldn't resist the thought of unknown treasures in a brown bag full of sight-unseen comics. Resisting such temptation was beyond the ability of a hapless eight-year-old boy.

I have to tell you, there was a lot of apprehension in a trade of that magnitude! Keeping the bag of comics hidden from Sister Ludgard was paramount to hiding a rodent in a field from an eagle at supper time. Somehow I survived the day, avoiding "the drawer" that had already claimed so many other items.

Planning, to a kid, isn't much fun, but making the trade on that Friday was serendipitous! The contents of the brown bag, as I discovered upon arriving home, included a consecutive run of comic books—not just any comic books, mind you, but Marvel comics, *The Amazing Spider-Man* to be exact! Those 12 cent wonders kept me holed up in my room for the entire weekend! I had never read a Spider-Man comic before, but once I did, I was hooked. And I haven't stopped yet! Written by Stan "The Man" Lee, with artists such as "Sturdy" Steve Ditko and "Jazzy" Johnny Romita, these books were candy for my mind, and I needed more.

One of the things that "The House of Ideas," better known as Marvel, knew back then was self-promotion! Page after page of brilliant comic book covers declaring daring exploits and extraordinary adventures just waited to be purchased—*Daredevil, Iron Man, the Hulk, Thor, Avengers, Fantastic Four*—you name it, all of them

AMAZING SPIDER-MAN #27, one of the many classic Spidey comics I acquired in my trade!

were "On Sale Now" for just twelve cents! By the end of that momentous weekend, my life had changed and my mind had reeled into a wonderful new world!

Entering into the world of comics presented two major problems—where was I going to find all of those comic books? and how, oh how, was I going to pay for them all? Finding them, it turned out, was simple. Paying for them was another story. Money was tight in those days, and even though twelve cents doesn't sound like a lot today, it was as close to a small mint as a young boy could ever imagine!

Marvel recognized the conundrum, as well. Kids just didn't have as much money to spend during the school year—but boy, did they have money during the summer months when even the lowest of jobs would pay enough to purchase a treasure trove of comic books! Mowing !awns, cleaning garages, picking up empty bottles—you name it, a dollar here, fifty cents there, and you had enough money to buy an entire week's worth of comics.

Taking advantage of kids that had money-that-would-burn-a-hole-in-your-pocket (one of my mom's favorite sayings), Marvel used the summer months to produce what they coined as summer annuals—double page giant-size comics that had kids drooling in anticipation. Of course, every title you collected had a summer annual, along with a regular monthly issue—and the annuals were twenty-five cents each!

And with the extra, giant-size comics, candy, and trading cards, it appears my mom was right—the money did seem to burn holes in our pockets!

ELMER'S GLUE

I'm about to discuss something that will either label me as being a strange, lonely child or just a normal kid growing up in the sixties who would do anything to amuse himself—depending on your point of view. I can't remember ever sharing this experience with my friends, so I don't know whether they were glue addicts like I was.

I loved Elmer's glue—the glue that goes on white, dries transparent, and was used for everything. I don't think a single day went by that we didn't construct something made with the glue. I'm not sure whether the school received some sort of kickback for the amount of glue used in a school year, but I know that we always seemed to have it around just in case a new art project were to arise.

One of my favorite pastimes was putting globs of glue on my fingertips and letting it dry to a transparent finish. Depending on the time of the year, it took a few minutes, a half hour, or even longer for the glue to dry. But after it did, I worked very hard at peeling it off my fingers. The goal was to remove each blob in one piece. If completed successfully, I had a perfect glue-mold of my fingerprints. I was fascinated by the procedure, but I know of no one else who ever did this—or at least ever admitted to doing it. To this day, I have no idea whether I was one strange kid or one of a legion of glue users who made duplicates of their own fingerprints.

YOU CALL THIS CANDY?

I think the big difference between growing up in the sixties and growing up today is this: Growing up today is to struggle toward adulthood in a world that has gone insane!

Need proof? Just today I read an article where U.S. candy makers are going to slim down their treats—that's right—candy—with no fat, no carbs—NO SUGAR? What!? As far as I'm concerned, they might as well call it something else. Call it anything but candy. In fact, they may have to. According to Webster's New World Dictionary, candy is described as "crystallized sugar made by boiling and evaporating cane sugar, syrup, etc." Further, it states, "candy—a sweet food, usually in small pieces or bars, made mainly from sugar or syrup, with flavoring, fruit, chocolate, nuts etc., added." Now that's candy!

But hey, all of that is about to change. Once again our youth are being robbed of their chance to indulge in a rite of passage as old as time itself! Candy without sugar? That's like Detroit announcing a new car that comes without an engine. I mean, come on, sugar-free Reese's™ Peanut Butter Cups? What's the point? You might as well just eat the wrapper the candy comes in.

Candy—I'll tell you all about candy. Most of it came loose and was sold in bulk! (gasp) I remember buying candy at Sage's store, right across from St. Stan's school, a cornucopia of sugar and fat and carbs—CANDY! Glass counters were filled with trays of bulk candy just ripe for the picking! A penny a piece, a nickel at most, and you could easily pack in enough candy to make your tummy hurt for a week!

I particularly remember the rock candy that basically looked like it sounded—glass-clear chunks of rocks looking like shiny diamonds just waiting to be mined—sugar diamonds mind you—pure sugar, and lots of it. I've got to tell you, if you were ten or under in the sixties, candy was your god and you were one of its worshipers.

Most of the candy, unwrapped and sold in bulk, became a real share-fest in some of the most unsanitary conditions known to man. Remember candy necklaces? Pure sugar beads strung on elastic that you wore around your neck. Yummy. I have to pause here to state that Shamokin was one of the most humid places I have ever lived in. Imagine a lazy, hazy, HUMID summer day, and you're running around with pure sugar strung around your neck! Imagine all of your buds stretching the elastic around your neck and biting off a mouthful of those sugar-morsels—man, candy never tasted better than that!

Another favorite was the UFO disks that looked just like they sounded—sugar wafers, saucer shaped, that had small beads of candy inside. The outer wafer would sort of melt on your tongue, much like the communion wafer the priest placed in your mouth at church on Sundays. In fact, I remember using the candy as a substitute for those wafers when we played church. Hey, when kids attended Catholic school, the boys all envisioned themselves becoming priests and the girls daydreamed about becoming nuns. Needless to say, I did not become a priest. In fact, I don't know of anyone in my school who did. But I digress!

Pixy Stix were one of the few candies that I remember coming in a package. A long, thin tube that resembled a straw that was filled with—you guessed it—pure sugar. Well, not pure sugar, I suppose, because there was also some sort of food color or dye that has probably long since been banned. Pixy Stix was another one of those sharing types of candy. Passing one around was a real treat…and another rite of passage. Just how much pure sugar could you fit into your mouth, and swallow, without getting really, really sick? In my mind the true definition of candy in the sixties would have been anything that contained pure sugar, and if consumed in sufficient quantity fast enough resulted in a diabetic coma!

WINDOW OF OPPORTUNITY

Squeaky brakes on a Tuesday morning were music to my ears. They belonged to the panel van driven by Mid-Penn News Agency's delivery person. The truck stopped once a week outside of St. Stan's School to drop off a bundle or two on the front step of Sage's, the family-run store that carried my favorite comic books! From my vantage point in the back row of the classroom, I was privy to all of the sights and sounds that put me in a Walter Mitty-like state.

Tuesday was special; the squeaky brakes, sliding panel door, and heavy bundle of books on the sidewalk meant one thing—the latest and greatest shipment of comic books had arrived. The downside was that time itself slowed down as I could see the bundle of goodies on the street two stories below me. I couldn't imagine that the hour or two between the drop off and lunch could move so slowly. Even worse for me was watching the bundle of comics sitting on the curb, waiting to be picked up and taken inside. I couldn't imagine how anyone in his right mind could leave those treasures sitting out on the front step for any length of time like an abandoned baby left behind in a basket on a doorstep.

Lunch never tasted as good as it did on Tuesdays. Eating as fast as I could, I made sure that I was the first one to make it over to Sage's to pick through the comics before anyone else could get to them. To my dismay, the books would often still be bundled and tucked away in the corner during my lunch hour. I wondered if Sage hadn't made some pact with the nuns not to sell any comics until the end of the school day.

ONE UP, ONE DOWN

As you may have noticed, one key component of growing up was the need to eat. And there was no better place to fill up than the Coney Island on Independence Street. The aroma wafted for blocks as though it had been sent by the food gods. I pictured the Coney Island as the place where these mythical creatures would eat if they walked the earth. Interestingly, Coney Island still exists to this day, and the place appears frozen in time as though wrapped with a spell of immortality that prevents it from ever going away.

What's so special about the Coney Island? To smell the aroma of onions cooking on a grill was enough to make you walk miles for their specialty. Imagine a restaurant surviving on exactly two items— hamburgers and hot dogs! These aren't just any dawgs and burgers, mind you, but the kind that melt in your mouth and still taste exactly the same today as they did decades ago.

"One up, one down" was the cry heard often at the Coney Island, their own language that conveyed the fact that they only had two items on the menu. Did I say menu? With only two items, there was no need for a menu. I always ordered the same, one up, one down. In a rare confession, I have to admit the only reason I ordered one of each was I never did know which was up and which was down. I didn't want to come across as being too stupid.

Okay, it might not sound like much. Hamburgers and hot dogs are nothing special—unless you're at the Coney Island in Shamokin! To order the delicacies any other way than their special way would be sacrilege—the hot dog, on a freshly steamed bun, with a daub of mustard, a special beef-based barbeque sauce, and finely chopped, raw onions—lots of onions—was a frankfurter connoisseur's dream. The burger was also a cornucopia for the taste buds—a grill-fried burger with a hit of mustard, the special barbeque sauce, and plenty of grilled onions. Wash it all down with an orange soda or a birch beer, and it was enough to make a dying man request the combo for a last meal.

A trip to town wasn't complete without a trip to the Coney Island! A hole in a wall by most standards, the store front had a neon sign announcing its presence—nothing else need be said. In fact, they really didn't need a sign to find the Coney Island. Once you were within a three block radius, you could follow your nose. The fact that the establishment still exists and still provides the best hamburgers and hotdogs found anywhere on the planet is testimony enough to the mouthwatering meal that awaits its patrons.

TRESPASSING ALLOWED!

Trespassing, stealing, and destruction of property were just some of the things that we did as kids to keep ourselves amused during the hot summer vacation. Of course, we didn't call it that back then. We called it playing. And the adults did, too!

Living in the Fifth Ward provided a plethora of amusement and entertainment. The neighborhood, occupied by predominantly lower income, hard working Polish and Italian families, was pretty self-contained as far as kids were concerned. Milk was still delivered to the front porch, and necessities like meat and bread were just a block away at Kolody's store. If a haircut was in order—Ted the Barber was just down the street! Everything a person could need was available on every corner of the Fifth Ward in the form of mom and pop storefronts that also served as their places of residency.

As far as playing was concerned, we had everything we needed within walking distance. Growing up on the south end of Shamokin Street was the perfect setting for pre-teen adventures. Every direction offered a new and different environment designed to provide big time entertainment!

Tonka trucks, the yellow replicas of big boys' toys in the form of dump trucks and steam shovels, ruled the sidewalks of the Fifth Ward! When we would collectively put our fleet of trucks together, we were a kiddie construction company in search of a construction site. That site, in the form of the local concrete redi-mix, was only a short wagon-ride away at the dead end portion of the street.

Looking back, I'm amazed to think about all those tons of

assorted gravel, sand, and other earthen supplies and thousands of dollars of heavy equipment that were parked out in the open—no fences or guards and no need for any!

Once the adults went home, the *real* work began! We inundated the massive stalls of sand, rock, and gravel, turning our Tonka trucks on the piles and digging tunnels and building roads. Working until dark (or until our parents called us for dinner), we wandered off, proud of a job well done. No one ever worked so hard at playing! Exhausted, sweaty, and hungry, we pushed our trucks home down the sidewalk (no one ever carried them, since they were, after all, *trucks*), hoping to avoid having to take a bath before dinner (even though we were covered in sand from head to toe). I doubt that anyone ever considered what we did back then anything more than clean, old-fashioned fun. Sure, we hauled off our fair share of sand and gravel in our wagons—and just the cuffed-up legs of my jeans held almost a sandbox full!

Many of our fellow co-workers on the "construction" site were our trusty green army soldiers. A lot of the toy soldiers ended up buried in caves dug in the sand with our mighty steam shovels and bulldozers. I often wonder how many of the loyal soldiers ended up as part of the sand/gravel mix in someone's patio or concrete walkway!

The gang of the Fifth Ward spent many happy hours working the giant wooden bins of sand and gravel at the concrete plant. And we learned quite a bit about the mixing of concrete and other construction-related skills. The collection of kids and toy trucks must have made an interesting sight to anyone looking in—like a colony of industrious ants building a new home. By today's standards we probably broke a lot of rules—and the concrete company no doubt violated a few more by just leaving us on the property—but that was the simplicity of growing up in the sixties. Life was uncomplicated, and kids were allowed to be kids!

GRANDMA'S HOUSE

One of the great things I remember from my childhood was going over to Grandma Novinskie's house—I didn't actually call her grandma, but rather Bushi, which I think was Polish for grandmother. The house, located on Pearl Street, sat about half way between my parents' house and St. Stan's school. It was semi-detached, which meant it had some space between it and the house next to it, unlike the typical row homes that were all attached within a single block of homes.

The front of the house faced Pearl Street and had a full length porch—ideal for sitting outside and doing nothing other than watching people walk by. The streets were so old that they were designed more for a horse and buggy than for automobiles. With cars parked on both sides, only one car could drive down the street at any given time, even though it was a two-way street! If a car headed down the street and another car headed up, it was often a matter of who was willing to back down, or rather back up, allowing the other car to pass.

Across the street was a warehouse that carried lumber and other construction supplies. Beyond that, a number of railroad tracks transported trains back and forth, night and day!

Once I walked through the door of my Bushi's house, the outside world melted away. Stepping through that door was like a trip back in time. Everything in the house was a generation removed from the latest and greatest advances that were starting to appear in kitchens and living rooms throughout the country.

43

And the smells—there was always something cooking on the stove at Bushi's house—morning, noon, and night. The smell would permeate the walls and floorboards, and food never smelled or tasted as good as what she prepared. In fact, my mom would tell me how people would comment on just how great the food smelled as they walked by the house on a Sunday morning after church.

Why wouldn't the food smell great? After all, it was prepared the old fashion way—on a coal stove, using the freshest of ingredients. In those days freshest ingredients didn't mean looking at the expiration date on the package—it meant *fresh*, as in straight from the back yard to the kitchen table! Sunday (after church) meant fresh chicken cooked Bushi's way! While we were at church, Grandma would go out to the back yard, grab a live chicken, behead it, pluck it, and prep it for the stove.

There was nothing quite as mouthwatering as a freshly cooked chicken! Bushi's kitchen was devoid of modern appliances, and even though cooking on a coal stove meant the temperature in the room rose to over one hundred degrees on a hot and humid summer day, no one minded! Smothered in butter and whatever secret ingredients she added, her special chicken made the tastiest meal ever prepared! I can't really recall what else was served, but I do know that I've never again tasted chicken cooked like that!

After dinner we sat around the radio, listening to old time music and the news. There was no television in the house—the radio ruled the roost! This was no ordinary radio—it was the size of a small refrigerator with double doors on the front that swung open to reveal giant knobs for volume and tuning in stations. Just turning the radio on was an experience—it had a warm up period before you could hear anything. The inside of the radio was a mix of wires and tubes glowing in an off-yellow hue that reminded me of a lab experiment gone wrong in Dr. Frankenstein's castle!

The rest of the house held many relics of a simpler time. The furniture was big and bulky, made of solid oak. The dining room table was especially intimidating—round and massive with giant legs with claw feet that made it look like it could get up and walk out of the room at any time!

Like most homes in Shamokin, the house was tall and longer

than it was wide. A typical home had four, sometimes five floors starting in the basement and ending in the attic. This particular basement was fairly big—by design. A giant coal furnace took up a lot of room. The front of the basement, facing the street, contained the coal shed. A small area, maybe ten foot by ten foot with a wooden wall and door served as the holding area for a ton or two of coal. A small window at street level served as the access for the delivery truck's coal chute. Since it was mined in abundance in the area, coal was the fuel of choice for heating and cooking back in the "good ol' days." It wasn't uncommon to see a coal truck pull up to the front of the house, open the window into the basement, place a coal chute between the truck and the window, and dump a full load of coal into the cellar. Most of the coal was pea coal or smaller so that it was easier to shovel into the furnace hopper—a giant bin that held enough coal to keep the furnace going throughout a cold winter's night.

Anthracite coal, unlike its rival, bituminous, burns very, very hot, but has too high an ash and sulfur content to be of much use in the steel-producing process. A home heated with a coal furnace was toasty warm during the most bitter of northeastern winters. It also had a sulfur smell that you never quite got used to and a thin layer of ash that covered everything in the house like frost blanketing the lawn on a brisk autumn day.

The other aftereffect of burning coal was taking out the ashes—a job that no one really seemed to want. If you put a lump of coal the size of your fist in the fire you were sure to get out a clinker—a hard cinder of ash—the same size as the lump of coal you put in the fire. There were so many clinkers of ash available that the city actually collected the ash to spread on the roads in the winter after one of the many heavy snowfalls that hit the town.

Climbing up out of the basement placed you smack in the middle of the first floor that consisted of a long hallway, a living room, dining room, and the kitchen, located in the back of the house. Climbing a flight of stairs led you to the third floor, where the bathrooms and bedrooms were located. A main bedroom at the top of the stairs and three other bedrooms towards the back, with the bathroom located between the two front bedrooms, rounded out the third floor.

A side door, off the back bedrooms, led to another flight of stairs. A short climb up the stairs revealed a single, large room that usually had sloped ceilings that matched the pitch of the roof. Since row homes and semi-detached homes had no garages, the attic became the storage place. If the family were large enough (people tended to have large families back then), the attic became the spare bedroom for the oldest kid, who no doubt wanted a little more privacy.

The backyard was another perk of days gone by—a large, covered porch with five or six steps led down to a grapevine-covered trellis that was large enough to hold a party underneath. The smell of grapes in the fall filled the air, and I often enjoyed cooling off on a hot day with a bunch or two of freshly picked grapes. The back of the yard was a mix of lawn and a small vegetable garden. The yard was long and narrow, the same configuration as the house (typical lots were two or thee times as long as they were wide). One of the treats was the cherry tree that the neighbors had in their yard. A bit of good fortune was the fact that the tree was massive and grew crooked— hence, limbs bearing cherries hung over into my grandmother's yard. As far as the neighbors were concerned, the cherries that were on our side of the fence were ours! I spent more than one day eating myself sick, my tummy overloaded with cherries, cherries, and more cherries! And nothing smelled better than a fresh-baked cherry pie, with homemade crust, right out of the coal oven!

Even though my Bushi lived only a few blocks from me, a trip to her house was always a feast for all of my senses—it was like a trip into the country rolled into a day in paradise!

SWIMMING LESSONS

Like so many great communities, Shamokin provided a number of diversions for summertime fun. One of the greatest summertime diversions was located at the west end of town, known as the Edgewood area. A sparkling clear lake, swimming pool, and enormous amusement park once made up that area, but by the time the sixties rolled around, the once great park had given way to Edgewood Gardens, a progressive, new subdivision of homes that featured large lots and state-of-the-art electric appliances.

But one of the park's greatest assets remained—the Edgewood swimming pool. Now this was not your ordinary, run of the mill swimming pool. This expansive pool of water had pedigree! The Edgewood pool had, in its heyday, the distinction of being the largest outdoor swimming pool in the state of Pennsylvania! I can only imagine there were a lot of grandiose pools throughout the state in communities much larger than Shamokin—but we had the largest!

Large was an understatement! As a kid I imagined the entire population of Shamokin could fit in the pool, and we'd still have room to swim around! Like a lot of things in Shamokin, it was a hand-me-down from my parents' generation—or before. The once great Edgewood swimming pool, while still impressive, was fast approaching its twilight years by the time my generation of kids dove in. But to us it was that oasis in the middle of the desert we knew as the hot, humid, blistering days of summer.

The pool itself was incredible—sparkling with cool water that appeared to be a football field long. The sides and bottoms were painted an aqua blue, giving the water the appearance of the tropical waters found in a peaceful, quiet lagoon located in the Bahamas or some other paradise. Three diving boards, two spring boards and a high dive tower, were located at the deep end of the pool—and it took an adventurous sort to even climb up the stairs to that high tower!

The author preparing to take a dip in
The Edgewood Pool circa 1963

One of the summer highlights for the neighbor kids was free swimming lessons. At least I remember them to be free. If there was a fee, it was nominal. As great as they were, the lessons did have one drawback; they were at seven a.m.—as in the morning! Don't get me wrong…getting up at seven o'clock was no big deal—the sooner we were up and about, the sooner we could start a fun-filled day of nothing but playing and horsing around. But man, I didn't know water could be that cold at seven o'clock in the morning, which was no doubt why the pool wasn't open to anyone else at that time of day. After all, who in their right mind would pay to turn their lips blue and to shiver non-stop for the rest of the day? But for the sake of learning to swim, we were there, Monday through Friday, ready to take the plunge in the icy waters in the hope of learning to swim.

Learning to swim was a secondary reason for taking swimming lessons. If you were going to partake of the Edgewood swimming pool, you had to learn to swim for survival's sake. The pool bottom wasn't made out of those fancy liners that today's pools are made out of, no sir! The Edgewood pool was made from concrete. Now I don't know when the pool was built, but I can only guess that concrete smoothing techniques had come a long way from those days. While the pool bottom looked inviting, painted with the enticing light blue colors, there wasn't enough paint at Jones Hardware Store to cover up the coarseness of the pool's bottom. If you ever make it to Hawaii and get the chance to walk over the hardened lava beds—do it with your shoes and socks off—and you'll begin to understand what it was like to walk on the bottom of the Edgewood swimming pool.

You didn't notice it so much when you were walking around in the pool all day because the water and chemicals sort of numbed your feet into shriveled up prunes. No, it was later in the day, when you were home, that you would notice all the cuts on the bottom of your feet—in some instances so bad that they would even bleed. And that's why every kid I knew braved the morning dip in freezing cold water to learn how to swim!

OUT OF THIS WORLD

Cowboys, Indians, gangsters, G-Men, soldiers—we all took our turn at playing the good guy or the bad guy. Sometimes it seemed that being the bad guy was a lot more fun than being the good guy all the time. What we learned was that it was the actual conflict—good versus evil—that drove all the imaginary games we played.

When the time came to play and we didn't want to be good guy or bad guy, we all played the same game—we envisioned being astronauts! If you were eight years old in 1966, then you were right in the middle of the most amazing race for space that the world had ever seen. Every kid I knew had the same dream of one day traveling to the moon and back!

The United States had been burnt by the Russians in the race to space with the launch of Sputnik, the first artificial satellite to orbit the earth. Given Americans' outright fear of Russia, the news of Sputnik gave the appearance of Russian supremacy over the United States. The fear became real panic when the Russians launched the first human being into space.

It took the assurances of President Kennedy that a man—not just any man, but a man from the United States—would set foot on the moon before the end of the decade. Not only was the United States striving to send man to the moon, but it was driven to do it before the Russians, who had a distinct advantage in the space race.

While President Kennedy didn't live long enough to see his promise fulfilled, it did indeed happen before the end of the decade— July 21, 1969 to be exact. I still remember the surreal scenes, sitting in my parents' living room and watching the blurry black and white images broadcast a quarter of a million miles away from on the surface of the moon. It was awesome to watch Neil Armstrong became the first person to set foot on another heavenly body. When he delivered his now memorable words—"…One Giant Leap for Mankind"— as he set foot on the moon, I realized it didn't matter who set foot on the moon first! The fact that human beings accomplished a task that was the stuff of science fiction a few short years before made it mankind's greatest accomplishment.

I remember being totally obsessed with space and dreaming of becoming an astronaut, even though I knew that with my grades the closest I was going to get to the moon was with my backyard telescope. I clipped every newspaper article I could find, and I followed the early Gemini missions with John Glenn as we worked our way towards the Apollo missions that would one day take us to the moon. I clipped all of the articles and taped them to my bedroom walls until there was no longer any room left. I even started to tape the clippings on the ceiling, covering every square inch except for the giant moon map that was directly over my bed. Every clear night, I would take my telescope (one of the coolest presents I've ever received) and peer out into space, looking at the craters on the moon and imagining a man one day setting foot on earth's only satellite.

Man's quest for space didn't come without a major cost of life. On January 27, 1967, three brave astronauts gave their lives in their quest for space. Apollo One was to test the giant Saturn booster rockets that would propel man past earth's gravitational pull and on to a rendezvous with the moon. Just before scheduled liftoff, a fire broke out in the main module where the astronauts were housed. Astronauts Grissom, White, and Chaffe died on the launch pad in that horrible fire. I will always remember that moment in time as my kids' generation will remember the Challenger Shuttle explosion.

Despite the tragedy, the Apollo missions moved forward, and I remember the night of the first moon orbit. It had taken ten more missions, but finally, with Apollo 11, we made it! It wasn't until years later that we all learned just how treacherous the trip to the moon was. In fact, while NASA and mission control were pretty confident that they could land on the moon, they weren't sure they could lift off of the moon, dock with the main capsule, and return to earth. Talk about all the excitement of a science fiction movie! Sometime later it was leaked that a speech had been written for President Nixon just in case we weren't able to bring back the astronauts. Thankfully, he never had to make that speech. The entire mission went smoothly, and man's trips to the moon became old news. With the apparent end to the space race, it seemed that there was no longer a real goal to keep going to the moon—as though the main incentive had been to beat the Russians and then call it quits.

Through it all I kept a keen interest in space and still have the three inch Tasco refractor telescope that my parents bought for me nearly forty years ago! Now I rarely find the time to venture outside on a clear night with that telescope, but when I do, I point it towards the moon, pick out a familiar crater or two, and think back to what it must have been like to set foot on earth's closest neighbor!

DOWNTOWN

Independence Street continues to be the main business district for the town of Shamokin. But back in the sixties (and before), the town was much more than a place to shop and conduct business. Independence Street was once a hustling and bustling downtown that served as a social gathering place. Presidential candidates made whistle stop train tours through town, and parades seemed to stretch for miles.

The eight or nine block area that made up Shamokin's downtown was an incredible mix of cars, pedestrians, and trains. The east end of town boasted a beautiful train depot, a typical train station of that day. The west end was capped with a park, complete with a memorial to fallen firefighters. In between the town had real character. Three movie theaters showed what are now considered classics, and the original five and dime, F.W. Woolworths, stood in the center of town. The equivalent of a modern-day Wal-Mart, the Woolworths store had anything and everything you could ever want. In fact, the lunch counter inside the store was a favorite spot for patrons to stop by for a cup o' Joe to discuss the weather, sports, or just about anything else.

Clothing stores, florist shops, professional businesses, hardware stores, and banks all thrived in the sixties. Cigar stores/newsstands could also be found up and down the street, and each of those stores—like Kleese's and Welker's—served up not only a plethora of comic books, newspapers, and magazines, but also their own soda counters. And, of course, Coney Island, which was always a required

53

stop if you were downtown, served as an anchor store. If you made the rounds up one end of Independence Street and down the other and you still had any change left in your pocket, you were obviously not doing it right!

Riding bikes served as our favorite way to get downtown. Back in those days, you could leave your bike outside the store and no one would ever think of stealing it. In the summer we would make several trips a week to town, but Tuesday was the day to go to town and get there early! All the new comics and magazines were put out on Tuesdays, with an added bonus of new record albums hitting the stores. Back then, buying 78 rpm records, or record albums as we referred to them, was all the rage.

A typical trip to town started with hitting three or four stores in search of the newest Marvel and DC comics. Between riding to town on our bikes and the exhilaration of new comics, we would always build up a big appetite—and that meant a trip to the Coney Island! Nothing hit the spot better on a hot summer day than a stack of new comics to read, a burger and dawg, and a birch beer to wash it all down!

Refreshed and ready to take on the rest of the town before heading back home, we would check out the latest record albums—the Beatles, Rolling Stones, Deep Purple—we bought them all. Before riding home, we always made sure we had more food for the rest of the afternoon. One of the stores that had the best deli counters downtown was the Jupiter store. Jupiter's was sort of an F.W. Woolworths wanna-be that had mostly clothes that were dumped in bins that sat in the middle of the floor. Everything in the store was arranged like a blue light special at K-Mart! I don't think I ever bought any clothes there, but I do remember the deli that was at the front of the store.

The deli had this great smell that assailed you as soon as you walked in. Their specialty was a basic sub sandwich—we called them hoagies back then—made of standard cold cuts. The real difference in their hoagies was the thinly sliced onions—I'm talking thinner-than-paper-you-could-see-through-them variety. In addition, they added just the right amount of Tabasco sauce on the bun! Add some lettuce, mayo, and tomato and you had a hoagie to die for! The hoagies, as I recall, were forty-nine cents, and we bought several at a time. The anticipation of getting home, putting on the latest records we had purchased, and reading the latest comics while chomping down on the best hoagie this side of Mac's hoagies was tough to beat! The combination of music, comics, and mouth-watering food was like a sensory-overload that made us wonder how we would ever make it until the following Tuesday!

Most of the fun we had growing up is no longer available in Shamokin, and it may have disappeared from other communities throughout the country. While Independence Street still serves as the main business district, a lot of its heart and soul is long gone. The train depot closed back in the sixties and was torn down to make room for a parking lot. Three movie theaters dwindled down to one, and for years the Victoria theater was the sole place in town to take a date to make out with in the balcony. The five and dimes, cigar stores, and soda fountains have all faded away, and comics are hard to find.

The one bright spot is that I can visit Shamokin today and make a pilgrimage to the still-great Coney Island—still on Independence Street in the same building where it has always been. Stopping by for a birch beer, burger, and dawg always makes my mind wander back to those days when Independence Street was a cornucopia of pleasures, a kids' fantasy come true!

MONEY MAKERS

I don't have the slightest idea how kids make money these days, especially when I see how expensive the things kids consider playthings are. Buying a game cartridge, DVD, or other form of entertainment today seems to take a small fortune. When I was growing up, even the smallest of jobs could earn one enough pocket change to purchase a wide variety of diversions—candy for a nickel, comics for twelve cents, trading cards for a nickel a pack—all inexpensive forms of entertainment.

Moving from Shamokin Street to Stetler Drive opened up a wide variety of business opportunities for an enterprising kid. First of all, the lots were big with large lawns that needed mowing—each and every week. It didn't take long to pick up one or two lawn mowing jobs per week. Sure it took an hour or longer to mow a lawn, but the rewards were worth it—I could easily make up to four or five dollars per lawn! Five dollars in the summer meant that I could buy all of the comics I could possibly want!

In fact, I think one of the benefits of growing up in the sixties and seventies was that we didn't have the entertainment distractions that kids have today! It's almost as though we're currently going through an entertainment overload! When I was small, I could buy every Marvel comic book that came out and still have money left over. And even when I bought every Marvel Comic every month, it still only amounted to a dozen or so books! I could easily find the time to read more—and wished there were more—but there weren't, and that's the reverse of today's entertainment options. In today's market I couldn't afford to buy every comic Marvel puts out on a monthly basis—well over one hundred titles, nor would I want to. If you multiply that number by the dozens of other comic book publishers today, it would be impossible to find the time to even read all of those books—much less have the money to buy them! Needless to say, they aren't twelve cents each anymore. The average comic book today costs two dollars and fifty cents!

Making money in the summer was a priority, and we had so many options! Mowing lawns opened a lot of doors for me—mostly garage doors! I had a regular job cleaning out the neighbor's garage. It was monotonous work, taking garage items out of the garage, sweeping it out, and putting everything back. Cleaning the garage was always good for a few extra bucks. The job became a regular weekly assignment, and not just in the summer months. Many years later I realized these people really didn't need to have their garage cleaned out each and every week, but they were kind enough to provide me with the busy work so I had a few extra dollars spending money. It was nice to know that we had such wonderful neighbors!

Practicing with the push mower on the grass in the backyard on Shamokin Street

One of my favorite ways to make a few extra bucks was hanging out at the Edgewood swimming pool, collecting glass soda bottles. A lot of the pool and the walkways were made of concrete, and the owners were paranoid about broken bottles and glass in and around the pool. Showing up early at the pool meant getting in for free, and we often stayed to hang out after our free swimming lessons. The operator of the soda counter would give us a wooden crate that had twenty-four slotted compartments made for collecting soda bottles. We would walk around the pool picking up empties and placing them in the case. Once the case was full, we took it back to the operator, who gave us a nickel and another empty case. On a busy, hot, humid day an ambitious kid could collect four or five cases in no time. I usually tried to work my way up to a buck in any given day and then call it quits by taking a refreshing dip in the pool.

I also did a little painting here and there to make some extra money, but I soon realized that painting was way too much work for me to want to do it on a regular basis. Through the summer I mostly stuck with cleaning garages, mowing lawns, and collecting bottles, content in the fact that I had enough spending money to purchase everything a kid considered to be essential for summer fun!

DOGGONE

One of my closest friends growing up on Shamokin Street was my English bulldog named Mitzy! I can't think of a better friend to have, for no matter where I went, the dog followed. Big and slobbery, Mitzy never left my side and let me torture her endlessly by pulling and prodding her whenever I felt like it. One of my favorite things to do was straddle the dog and ride her like a cowboy on a bucking bronc. That's how I remember it in my childlike fantasies. The reality of it all was that, if you know anything about an English bulldog as a breed, you know their favorite thing to do is sleep. Describing riding Mitzy around like a wild bronc is like describing watching paint dry as an extreme sport. I mostly sat on top of her, whooping and hollering while she lay prone on the floor—but I have to tell you, it sure was a lot of fun!

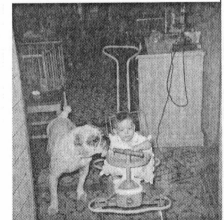

A boy and his dog—does it ever really get any better than this?

59

Loyalty, on the other hand, is a trademark of the breed, and I loved that dog as much as a little kid could. In fact, I grew to love that dog so much that the bulldog became my favorite breed of dog. Thanks to my wife, I still own a bulldog today—Xena, Warrior Bulldog! Brindle in color, she is as close to reliving my childhood years with Mitzy as I'll ever get.

Unfortunately, Shamokin Street was fraught with dangers for cats and dogs alike. I was just old enough to understand that my faithful companion was gone one day—just gone! But I wasn't old enough to understand that she was never coming back. I can't remember what my parents told me, but I remember it was something comforting so that I didn't feel quite so bad about Mitzy's absence. It wasn't until years later that I found out the truth. Mitzy had become very sick, and my parents were afraid to let me near her. I believe some friends took her out to a farm to live out whatever days she had left. I know that my parents did the right thing, but I sure wish I could have said goodbye!

Like most kids, I got over things quickly, and nothing says happy like a new puppy. A bright eyed, black and white Boston Terrier—my second favorite dog in the world—came to live with us! Porky was his name, but don't blame me because I'm pretty sure my parents came up with that moniker. Porky turned out to be a very faithful dog—every bit as faithful as Mitzy. Unfortunately, Shamokin Street once again proved fatal to my four legged companion. I remember my aunt, who was a nurse, visiting at the time, and there was an awful screech in the street. Everyone ran out of the house and onto the sidewalk to see what our hearts had already told us—Porky had been hit by a car. I remember Porky lying on the sidewalk with blood coming out of his mouth and ears. His breathing was hard and irregular. My aunt took his pulse, but it didn't take a nurse to tell me that I was about to lose another favorite pet. As much joy and wonderment as they bring to people, I sometimes wonder if dog ownership is worth it. It's always so unbearable when the treasured pet ends up dying.

SNOW DAZE

When you're ten, there are no greater words than SNOW DAY! By the time winter had crept into the school year, we were all getting a bit crazy. Thankfully, we lived in a part of the country that had snow like Florida has oranges! The snow could start in October and continue well into April. I recall my parents telling me how they walked blocks and blocks to school in knee-deep snow. You know what? I never doubted that.

A snow day was something that we all looked forward to—that is, the kids did. Snow for adults meant extra work and a lot of headaches. Snow for kids meant a day off from school and waxing the runners on our sleds so that we could hit Mulberry Hill at first light. The greatest snow day was one that happened on the day of a major exam at school. How much did we count on a snow day? We would sit in front of the radio and listen to all of the weather forecasts that were tracking the storm. We soon learned the difference between a winter storm watch and a winter storm warning (a watch meant it might snow, but a warning meant snow was imminent). Snow days were built into the local school district calendar, and it was almost impossible to make it through a winter without a single snow day. The chatter would start the day before at school, where kids would talk about early reports of snow while making plans to rendezvous at the local ski hill. Later that evening the radio would broadcast snow warnings with accumulation predictions. If we were lucky, it would start to snow before bedtime so that school would be cancelled before we were tucked in. Canceling school the night before allowed for a good night's sleep, secure in the knowledge that the morning, which should have been spent in school, would instead be spent at the sled run. Now that was about as good as it got!

If we went to bed with visions of snowflakes dancing in our heads, we headed to the window the first thing when we got up to see just how much snow we had received. I have to tell you that there was no greater disappointment than going to bed with predictions of a foot or more of snow by morning, only to wake up to bare, dry ground. I often wonder how many kids took a sick day after being disappointed by a no-show snow day.

There was nothing quite like building
a snowman with Mom after a big snow!

Thankfully, from a kid's point of view, the weather forecasts were seldom wrong. In fact, there were a lot of times when the snow accumulation amounts were underestimated. Snowfalls in the one to two foot range weren't uncommon.

Snow caused major problems in Shamokin—the streets, especially in the Fifth Ward, were so narrow that snow made getting around difficult. Given the fact that row houses, which were common throughout town, were so narrow, the parking place in front of each one wasn't much longer than the length of your car. Many adults would shovel out their cars in order to get to work, throwing the snow into the street and making driving extra hazardous. One of the traditions in Shamokin—and I've never seen this anywhere else—was to place something in your vacated parking place in front of your house so that—after a lot of hard work shoveling out—no one else would park there! I've seen people put their kitchen table and chairs in the street curbside to keep someone else from parking there. Driving up Shamokin Street after a blizzard looked like a giant neighborhood yard sale with every known piece of household furniture lining the streets to save parking spots.

One of the more interesting aspects of snow removal was the use of front end loaders and dump trucks. The snow would be plowed into large piles and loaded in to dump trucks to end up being dumped into Shamokin Creek. It really was the most economical and logical way to clear out massive accumulations of snow. After roads were opened and snow packed, the city would spread coal ashes on the streets in order to add traction for vehicles that ventured out into the weather. For several days the fresh-fallen snow added a white contrast to the black and white surroundings that were the trademark of this coal mining community. There was nothing like the fresh-fallen snow— the peace and solitude it offered was unlike any other sight in the world.

GAME NIGHT

Growing up in Shamokin meant one thing when it came to baseball—The Philadelphia Phillies! Everyone I knew was a Phillies fan—except for me. I was a closet Pittsburgh Pirates fan. And why not? Guys like Clemente and Stargell made for modern day heroes. Being a Pirates fan in a town dominated by Phillies fans made life simpler when it came to trading baseball cards. I would gladly surrender my Phillies cards for those of Pirate players. I always ended up with the sweet end of the deal since I could often get two or three Pirates for one good Phillies card.

Since we were geographically closer to Philadelphia, the local radio station—WISL—covered all the Phillies games on the radio. Day or night, I can remember listening to Phillies games broadcast over our local radio station. Since my bedtime was early, I often had to beg to be able to stay up long enough to listen to a complete game. After all, there's no point in listening to a baseball game for six or seven innings and then turning it off. The compromise was that I had to be in bed, but I could listen to the game on my transistor radio using an earpiece.

One of two things happened then. I would fall asleep in the later innings, not knowing who had won. Or else I'd make it through an entire game—especially if it was a tight game in the last few innings. I most enjoyed the games that the Phillies played on the west coast. Given the three hour time difference between the west and the east coasts, a seven o'clock start in Los Angeles meant a ten o'clock start back home. I had a tougher time convincing my parents to let me stay up that late, but I usually won out since they figured I would doze off long before the game was over. Thinking back, I'd have to say that I was probably batting about .500 as far as staying awake was concerned.

I remember a few times that either the Phillies or Pirates were in the playoffs, a special time for baseball fans. The only problem was that, back in those days, baseball was played for the players and not television ratings. This meant a lot of great playoff games were broadcast while I was in school. To hear them, I had to sneak a transistor radio with earpiece into school and listen to it during class without getting caught. The real trick was to never turn the volume up any higher than needed to barely hear the game. I listened to a lot of baseball during school time, and I never got caught!

DONUT DAY

Donut Day at Saint Stan's was one of the biggest days of the year. The cafeteria workers would make hundreds, maybe thousands of donuts for the occasion, and they would be miraculously gone by the time the last bell rang at the end of the day. People would put in orders months in advance, a dozen here, three dozen there. I had no idea that so many cake donuts could be consumed in one day.

Nor do I have any idea where, when, or why the idea of Donut Day got started, but I'm pretty sure that it became a huge money maker. Arriving at the school on Donut Day was another one of those special events that marked the privilege of growing up in the sixties in Shamokin. If you can picture a kid eating all the donuts he can hold and washing them down with chocolate milk, then you can picture Donut Day from a kid's point of view. All I cared about was that I had enough money in my pocket that day to buy all the donuts I could possibly eat! I don't want to say I ever overate my share of cake donuts, but I will say that Donut Day was always followed by another special day at school. It was called a sick day!

THE VICKY

By the time I was old enough to attend movies by myself, Shamokin was down to one remaining movie theater. The Majestic, which was once next to the Victoria, and the Capitol (where the Wendy's is on Independence Street today) were both torn down years earlier. The Victoria, or Vicky as locals called it, was a grand old movie house with a main floor and balcony. The screen was large, much bigger than the ones found in today's multiplexes, and the popcorn was popped fresh with real butter as the topping. The candy counter displayed large-sized boxes of sweets that would last through an entire movie.

The Vicky was a classic movie theater in every sense of the word. The outside marquee lit up and had giant, red plastic letters that displayed the name of the movie playing. The outside display cases were made of glass and had light bulbs on the side that lit up the "Now Playing" movie poster. The theater also had an outside display for lobby cards—full-color stills of scenes from the movie. A person could spend a lot of time looking over the stills to get a feel for the movie that was playing. The outside of the building had a large number of glass display cases to hold the "Coming Soon" posters you could view as you drove down the side street.

Movies were seventy-five cents, with the added bonus of being able to stay in the theater after the movie was over and watch the next screening—without paying again! Not only was staying for a movie twice the norm back then, it was encouraged by management. (The longer you stayed, the more candy and soda you would buy.)

Another wonderful aspect of the Vicky was the Saturday afternoon matinee. The matinees always featured movies geared towards kids. I think the concept of the matinee was that parents could drop off their kids, do some shopping downtown (while getting a break from their kids), and then pick them up on the way home.

An incentive to be there for the matinee was the intermission, when the manager would go up on stage and draw tickets stubs to give away door prizes. There was always excitement in the air at intermission time. Prizes were placed in brown paper grocery bags and consisted of three or four toy items. The girls would win a doll and some dresses, and the guys would get a toy gun or G.I. Joe or some other similar guy-thing.

Because the Vicky was a really, really old movie theater, it had a history. I had heard tales from my parents and grandparents about when real live theater was performed on the stage. I recall stories about Vaudeville performers passing through town and trying out their acts on the "tough coal miner crowds" of Shamokin. Often I heard that if an act survived Shamokin, it could make it anywhere. I was much too young to ever see any of these acts, but I could just imagine an earlier time when an act would come through town, possibly by train, do a performance or two, and then head out for the big city. It must have been an exciting time to visit the Victoria Theater!

In the 1960s the movie rating system was still in the future. All of the movies were good, wholesome pictures that a family with kids could see. In fact, many of today's classics played a major role in the success of the theater. As I grew a little older, I do remember some sort of movie rating was put in place. I recall an "M" rating for mature audiences, but I don't ever recall seeing that type of movie at the Vicky.

The Vicky was divided into two areas, the first floor where the parents and kids sat, and the balcony, where the older kids took their dates to watch the movie—and maybe steal a kiss or two from their sweethearts!

I can only ever remember seeing one movie at the Capitol, I think it was the *Ten Commandments*, after which the theater closed. Every other movie I saw was at the Vicky. I spent so much time at the Vicky that, during my high school years, I ended up working as an usher, ticket collector, and candy/popcorn vendor. It was a dream job since I got to see many of my favorite movies—over and over again! I even ventured to the back rows of the balcony, usually with girls that I let in to the movies for free. But I suppose that's a tale for another book!

One of the best kept secrets about the Vicky was a back room located on the same level as the projection room. This room was barren except for a table, chair, cot, and shelves filled with stacks and stacks of movie stills and movie posters. My guess would be that the room had thousands of posters and stills dating back to the early days of movies. I think the posters actually went back to the days of silent movies! I do remember seeing the poster and stills for *Gone With the Wind* and being thoroughly impressed. That room was like a movie buff's wildest dream come true! I have no idea as to what ever happened to all those movie posters, but I'm pretty sure that, as scarce as most of them were, they had to be worth a small fortune. Where they've gone is probably a mystery that will remain unsolved forever.

In the last handful of years, the Vicky fell victim to progress and was torn down after several failed attempts to rescue and restore it to its glory days. It is indeed sad to consider that a movie house that was once as grand as the Vicky—with ties to Vaudeville and the early days of Hollywood—has forever disappeared from the lives of the kids of Shamokin!

FIRE STATIONS

Sometimes, growing up in a certain environment leads one to simply accept the way in which things are done. I've noticed that in particular about some of the social functions and customs unique to Shamokin.

The strangest thing I remember was the way in which the volunteer fire stations were run. Now I think everyone would agree that we had some of the best fire stations and firefighters you could find—dedicated men (I don't remember women being allowed on the fire teams back then) who took their business of firefighting very seriously. The Rescue and the Independence Hose Companies were two of the best! Given that row homes were notorious for burning down entire blocks of connected housing and that some of the homes in Shamokin were so old that they'd never pass new wiring and building codes, I was surprised we didn't have more serious fires. And that was due to the quick response of the firefighters that manned the fire houses.

But there seemed to be this secret society involved with joining a fire company in Shamokin. If you were Catholic, you could only join certain fire companies, the same for the Protestants. Some fire companies made exceptions, but you could never, ever hold an office or rank within that organization. Shamokin had no paid firefighters, so I suppose they could make up whatever rules they wanted. But I still don't understand why a religious preference made one eligible or ineligible for a fire department. Maybe the Catholics used holy water to put out the fires—who knows?

70

An even more bizarre aspect of many fire stations was their function as a social gathering place. Only members could get in, or someone who was a friend of a member. And what would one do at the fire station? Most fire stations had huge halls for gatherings that included a place to serve food, several dart boards, and, of course, pool tables. Some even had pinball machines and, rumor had it, honest-to-goodness slot machines. My understanding was that a lot of the married guys joined the fire stations in order to have a place to get away from their wives. Did I mention the fact that some of the fire stations had strict rules? For example, if you were a member, you had to take turns each week tending bar. Yep, I said bar! Many, if not all, the fire stations in Shamokin had large bars that served draft beer—usually at a discount to members—ten cents a tall glass, as I recall. I don't know about anyone else, but I find it odd that a fire station, staffed with volunteer firefighters, would allow the firefighters to drink while in the station.

I also heard tales of members having quite a few drinks under their belt when the fire alarm would sound—the mantra of the time being that, once the alarm sounded, everyone sobered up in a hurry. I don't know how that worked, and I don't know how they got away with it from a legal point of view (driving a fire truck, intoxicated, to the scene of a fire?). Needless to say, growing up in that environment meant that no one ever questioned the practice, and it was the norm for fire stations, not only in Shamokin, but also quite a few of the surrounding counties.

Whenever I recount these stories to outsiders, they look at me in disbelief and dismiss the stories as just that—stories. For those of us who grew up in Shamokin, we know that the stories are much more than that—they are fact. The other fact that remains is that, no matter how contradictory the working conditions at the volunteer fire stations sounded, everyone slept well at night knowing their homes were being protected by their family and friends and that when a fire broke out, everyone gave a hundred and ten percent.

WIFFLE BALL

Baseball is indeed the National Pastime. For the gang of the Fifth Ward, there was no better game than baseball. Any empty lot would do as a field, with pieces of cardboard serving as bases. All we needed was a ball, a bat, and few gloves. Back then, not everyone could afford baseball gloves, so we always shared our gear.

Even with seven or eight kids, we could get together a pick up game of baseball. The sport was fun to play and the rules were simple. We chose sides, and it didn't matter who was better at baseball because we always picked our best friends to be on our side. If we ended up with an odd number of players, we would use one pitcher for both sides—often the oldest kid in the group because he (or she) was the only one who could pitch the ball over the plate with any consistency. Boys and girls both played back then. We didn't exclude girls from playing because without the girls, we wouldn't have enough kids to even play the game.

Rarely did we keep score since the overall purpose of playing baseball was hanging out and getting together with as many kids in the neighborhood as possible. Baseball was one of the few games we could play that everyone could participate in—especially if everyone showed up at the field. We always tried to make sure that everyone got a chance to bat, and almost everyone got a hit and a chance to run around the bases—even if it meant lobbing the ball in a slow, high arc over the plate. There wasn't a lot of competition with our baseball games—unless you counted who was having the most fun.

One of the greatest inventions of our time was the wiffle ball and bat—a long plastic bat with a plastic ball, usually with holes in it. The holes in the ball were really great because you could make it curve if you got just the right amount of spin on it. The added bonus was that the ball made some really cool whistling noises as the air rushed through it.

Wiffle ball was a great game. It was played just like baseball but on a smaller scale. The ball wouldn't travel quite as far as a hard ball, which was a good thing since most of the areas we played base-ball in weren't regulation size baseball fields.

The plus was that, no matter how hard the wiffle ball was hit, it rarely traveled very far. And no matter how hard the ball was hit, you could get whacked with a line drive and feel a little sting and end up with a little red mark—as opposed to getting hit with a hard ball that really hurt and left a major bruise, or worse!

The real simplicity of the wiffle ball and bat was that you could play an entire game without the need for baseball gloves. Depending on who would show up at the field for a game, we sometime didn't have enough gloves for the team on the field. And that made it a bit tough to field line drives and deep fly balls. With wiffle ball the rule of thumb was that we would play without gloves so that every-one had a fair chance. Catching a hard hit fly wiffle ball was the equivalent of throwing a hard ball straight up in the air and catching it with your bare hands.

Hard ball or wiffle ball, it didn't matter—what did matter was that all of the kids in the Fifth Ward had the opportunity to get together and play. Whether you were young or old, boy or girl, hav-ing fun didn't discriminate!

Baseball was a theme that carried over long after I moved from Shamokin Street to Stetler Drive. Now that we were a little older, everyone had, at a minimum, a baseball glove. Making new friends in a new part of town was easy as long as you had a ball, a bat, and a baseball glove. For us older kids, the game was becoming a little more involved. I had actually gone from owning the little plastic gloves that kids had to a real leather glove complete with the name of a professional baseball player engraved right in the leather. In fact, it was after my move to Stetler Drive that I realized there was more than one type of baseball glove. I soon encountered a catcher's mitt and a first baseman's glove!

Best of all, we discovered our own field of dreams right in my very back yard! Living on the south side of Stetler Drive meant that our back yard faced property owned by the Shamokin Area School District. Just across the road from my back yard was a giant field, not an ordinary field, but a green, grass-groomed baseball field with a fenced backstop! It even had real bases evenly spaced out with a real mound for the pitcher to stand on! Best of all, it was just sitting there—no fence, no admission fees, no guards to tell you to go away, an honest-to-goodness baseball field just waiting to be played on.

Stelter Drive in the sixties was like a maternity ward with kids popping up every other day! Still enforcing the girls-can-play-rule, we were now able to get enough kids to field two full teams! And we had equipment—any number of bats to choose from and balls numbered in the double digits! We had a well-staffed baseball team—with nobody but ourselves to play! But that's okay, because like the gang from the Fifth Ward, our real goal on a hot, hazy summer day was nothing short of having fun playing the great American Pastime!

TRANSPORTATION

Every kid had some form of transportation. Given that cars were just starting to proliferate, we could still ride our bikes up and down the street without much hesitation. Our modes of transportation were simple back then—scooter, skateboard, wagon or bike—pretty similar to what kids use today—only without all the bells and whistles.

My bike in the late sixties was a black Schwinn™, and as far as I could tell, that was the only bike made at the time. Big and bulky, it weighed more than I did, so you were careful not to have it fall on you or else you'd be stuck! It also only had one speed—and that was as fast as you could pedal. No shifters, no derailleur, just a chain with a large sprocket in the front and a smaller one in the back. No hand brakes either—back then bikes were simplicity itself. Pedal forward to go forward, and pedal backward to stop. It didn't get much simpler than that. Accessories consisted of a small, round mirror that attached to the handlebars and two rubber hand grips that slid over each end of the handlebars (complete with plastic streamers that sounded cool in the wind).

Bikes were just something that every kid was expected to own. As long as I could remember, I had a bike of some sort, starting with a sleek, red tricycle. Every kid had a tricycle—one wheel in front and two in the back. The back of the bike had a foot base that older kids could stand on and help push you up a big hill if your legs weren't strong enough to pedal to the top.

Somewhere between the tricycle and training wheels, we had

the pedal car. Pedal cars were cooler than cool. Made of rugged cast iron or some similar metal, the push car looked like a miniature version of the car your dad drove (okay, it didn't, but to a five-year-old, it did). The push car had four tires and a steering wheel and you actually sat in the driver's seat, just like a regular car. The inside of the car had two push pedals that you put your feet on. The harder and faster you pushed the pedals back and forth with your feet, the faster the car went. Pedal cars were great, and as an added bonus, the wheels, axles, and frames usually served as the framework for soapbox derby race-type cars that the older kids would build.

My first bike—a tricycle, circa 1962!

Somewhere between that tricycle and push car came the training wheels. Training wheels were two smaller wheels that attached to the rear of a two-wheeled bicycle. It wasn't an uncommon scene to see a parent running down the sidewalk next to a bike with a kid on it who was trying to ride a two-wheeler with training wheels. It seemed like some strange sort of ritual that adults felt obligated to carry out. Given the progression of vehicles we had as kids, it seemed more than logical that we would have been able to figure out how to ride a two-wheeler on our own. But for some reason, that one moment in time—that connection between adult and child—was something that became a lasting memory for adults. Who doesn't remember teaching his or her kids to ride a bike?

Strange as it may sound, no kid ever remembers the exact moment when they crossed over from four wheels to two wheels. The reason, of course, is simple. The training wheels, like some giant crutch, stayed on the bike long after they were needed. Training wheels would often loosen and shift position so that, at times, one or none was touching the ground. It got to the point where they no longer touched at all, and that was when we were really riding a two wheeler. The training wheels were just along for the ride!

Bikes in those days were no big mystery. As long as the chain stayed on the sprockets and you kept it well oiled, the bike would go on and on! Even the tires were tougher than tough, and flats were few and far between. No matter how hard you rode your bike, the thing would never break down. Even if the chain did loosen and fall off, it was a simple procedure for a kid to put it back on!

One thing still puzzles me about bikes though—it's the stabilizer bar that goes from the seat to the yoke of the handlebars. Somewhere in the annals of history, I'm pretty sure that things got mixed up. The boy's bike had the bar that was attached just below the seat. If you ever took a hard hit or had a sudden stop on your bike and came off your seat to land on that bar (and you were a guy), you know what I'm talking about. Having that bar hit your groin was enough to ruin your best day. And then there's the girl's bike—same bar, only it starts out from the handle bar yoke but curves downward to the bottom of the bike near the chain. What's up with that? I would have preferred to have a girl's bike for that very reason, but things like that just weren't done in those days. All I know is that if someone did enough research, we'd find out that somehow the blueprints for bikes were switched, and that girls' bikes should really be the boys' version.

SICK DAYS

Sick back in the sixties and sick today have very different meanings. Back in the sixties, being sick meant that you really had to be at death's door to even come close to staying home from school. Today, taking a sick day just means you just don't want to go to work or school. Sure, there are legitimate reasons for being sick and staying home today, but back in the sixties, staying home because you were sick came with dire consequences!

Don't misunderstand. There was no greater feeling than staying home from school when you felt perfectly fine! Faking an illness was a great way to be pampered by Mom with food and juice in bed and, if you were lucky, being allowed to spend the day on the couch in front of the television. My favorite version of the sick day was to pick a day when I had a really big test that I failed to study for. There was also a special feeling if the day turned out to be rainy and extra gloomy. If I couldn't go out and play at the end of the school day because I was "sick," I took satisfaction in knowing that even the kids that had gone to school couldn't go out and play either. It wasn't a matter of being mean or vindictive, but rather a joy in knowing that I got away with staying home all day without missing any play time!

I mostly enjoyed the feeling of being able to stay home for no particular reason other than I said that I didn't feel well. Between watching television and reading comic books, a faked sick day was like an adult vacation day on a kid's level!

As we would later learn in school, for every action there was an equal and opposite reaction—and that reaction usually came in the form of Grandma! There were inherent risks involved with faking a sick day. In fact, I can recall many a time when I actually went to school sick because I feared one of Grandma's home remedies. Her home remedies were not to be mocked—they did, in fact, seem to work, defying every Hippocratic oath ever uttered.

Just thinking about one of Grandma's remedies was enough to instantly cure any ailment I might have. I guess there is something to be said for mind-over-matter!

Some of the remedies were pretty common, and I'm sure that every kid alive has endured at least one of them. If you had a sore throat, you had to take a big tablespoon of castor oil—sort of like swallowing motor oil that had been drained out of an Edsel! If the sore throat was extreme, it meant, gulp, a second tablespoon! Announcing a sore throat on a school day in front of Grandma meant one of two things—either go to school or swallow the castor oil! A chest cold meant having your chest smeared with Vicks VaporRub™ and then having your chest covered with a diaper while being tucked in bed under a two thousand pound down blanket. After all, the only way to break a chest cold was to sweat it out, followed by a hot shower to close those pores in the morning.

One of the strangest remedies (and the one we most avoided) was the follow-up cure for a sore throat—and that was being forced to eat Vicks VaporRub™! I don't know which was worse, the feel of the greasy, slimy, mentholated rub hitting the back of your throat or the vision of Grandma sticking those two crooked, old fingers in the jar and telling you to open wide. I still shudder and break out into a cold sweat when I pass the Vicks section in the grocery store. (It's worthy of mention here that the Vicks website states clearly that this product is for *external use only*! Too bad Grandma didn't read that.)

Parents also had a litany of preventative methods for colds that were used as either warnings or excuses if you did catch cold. At my house it was impossible to make it out the front door without being asked if I had my hat on, and whether or not I was wearing a t-shirt—as if wearing a t-shirt was ever going to prevent a cold. The big concern was always whether or not I was going out with my hair wet. Everyone knows that going out with your hair wet causes colds, or worse! Hmmmm. I wonder how they felt about the virus theory as the cause of the common cold. I also wonder if bald people caught more or fewer colds due to the absence of hair.

Sometimes, no, most times the home remedies were much worse than the illness. Faking a sick day had perilous consequences that few kids dared! When we were sick, it often meant going to school rather than making a big deal out of it! Sure, Mom's chicken soup was always a welcome sight when you had a serious cold, but facing any of the other home remedies was enough to make sure we tried our best to stay healthy!

HARD OR SOFT?

One of the biggest debates to rage in the confines of five- to ten-year-old age bracket was which was better—hard or soft ice cream? We had plenty of options for ice cream, and it was an ongoing process to determine which was better.

One of the favorite places in all of Shamokin (and not just for kids, but adults, too) was Martz's ice cream located on West Arch Street. All of their ice cream was made fresh in the store, and there was no better treat than buying a full scoop of hard ice cream for ten cents—fifteen cents would get you a double scoop. Martz's had, without a doubt, the best hard, hand scooped ice cream in town!

Martz's also had a great soda counter where you could go in and order a root beer float, milkshake, hot fudge sundae, banana split, or any other ice cream treat you could ever imagine. The stools were those pedestal types with round seats cushioned with padded plastic tops that spun around and around.

Large, glass cases held containers of ice cream with at least a dozen on display at any given time. People came from all over to pick up a delicious cone filled with their favorites. For me it was chocolate or chocolate chip. The chocolate was rich and dark, and the chips were so big that they crunched in your mouth as you bit down on the ice cream! There's just something about natural homemade-style ice cream on a hot summer night that no other experience can ever measure up to.

On the other hand, when we had our fill of hard, hand scooped ice cream, we had the option of some of the best soft serve ice cream to ever come out of an ice cream dispenser. And best of all, we had daily summer delivery of ice cream right to our front door!

If you grew up without ever experiencing first hand the wonders of a Mister Softee ice cream truck pulling into your neighborhood, you just didn't have much of a childhood! Mister Softee, a large truck with a generator and giant ice cream cones with smiley faces on the front of the truck, magically appeared in our neighborhood every summer, only to disappear in the winter like a bear heading into hibernation!

As far as soft serve ice cream goes, Mister Softee had two flavors, available in three variations—chocolate, vanilla, and chocolate/vanilla twist. I was partial to the twist ice cream cones since you could give you tongue a real treat by alternating licks between the vanilla and chocolate! Sundaes were also a Mister Softee staple—typically hot fudge sundaes with whipped cream, nuts, and a cherry on top, or the really decadent marshmallow crème sundae—vanilla ice cream with marshmallow crème, nuts and a cherry! We always made sure that we planned our outdoor play periods around the arrival of the Mister Softee truck.

Sadly, Martz's in its original form, ceased to exist quite a few years ago. And while I haven't had a soft serve ice cream from a Mister Softee truck in decades, I hear rumors that they still exist. Just once I'd love to walk out my door on a summer day and hear the musical announcement of the Mister Softee pulling up in front of my house for one more dish of soft serve ice cream—complete with whipped cream, nuts, and a cherry on top!

.

PIZZA

Is there a food greater than pizza? While it comes in all shapes and sizes, there seemed to be a proliferation of pizza perfection within a ten mile radius of Shamokin. We had James' and Mr. Pizza, while Marion Heights had the Tower of Pizza, or Dukes, as the locals referred to it.

When it comes to pizza, I'm not talking about the chains that produce generic stuff that tastes identical to all other pizza. No, I'm talking about the type of pizza unique to a particular establishment that used its own recipe containing some closely guarded secret ingredients! Okay, Mr. Pizza on Spruce Street was nothing more than a carryout joint that had cookie cutter pizza—but was it ever good! Not good like the best pizza your taste buds ever tasted, but rather a unique taste that was consistent in quality—the type of taste that you never let yourself forget and can't go for more than a week without.

The uniqueness of Mr. Pizza was that it made only one type of pizza—pepperoni—and there was always a hot slice waiting for you when you walked in the door. The pizzas were large, rectangular pies baked in big gas ovens. A sweet sort of sauce was place on top of the dough with grated cheese—and then each piece was topped off with exactly one nickel-sized piece of pepperoni. When sliced in equal square pieces, each pizza pie would produce a pizza masterpiece! Always hot and fresh, every piece was pizza-perfect! On a good night one could easily eat seven or eight pieces.

There was a certain knack to ordering at Mr. Pizza that was akin to ordering soup from the soup Nazi from a Seinfeld episode! A person would walk up to the counter, tell the clerk how many slices he or she wanted, and then step to the side so the next person could order. It was a simple procedure that worked for decades. The best thing about Mr. Pizza is that it is so good that nothing has ever changed. The store still stands today, providing testament that good pizza is good pizza.

The true test of pizza is, of course, how good it tastes cold the next morning. The hardest thing about eating hot Mr. Pizza was exerting enough will power to save a few pieces for the next day!

One has to remember that, in the sixties, restaurants in Shamokin were family run establishments that produced quality food from scratch—fast food had yet to overrun our small community. No McDonald's, no Pizza Hut™, nothing but home cooked meals that have withstood the test of time.

There was a local battle of wills in Shamokin concerning the best pizza in a sit down environment—James' in Shamokin or Duke's in Marion Heights. Think Betty versus Veronica or Ginger versus Maryanne, and you'll understand the battle lines drawn between these two establishments. They had similarities. Both were located on the corner and were part restaurant, part living quarters, with a full-service barroom.

It could even be stated that the pizzas were very, very similar. Baked square, they could be ordered as half of whole pies. If you ordered a whole pie, you actually received two halves. The crust was very thin and had a special crunch to it. Both sauces were very unique, only to be outdone by the cheeses. I can only imagine what type of cheese they used—I never got up the nerve to ask because I had heard that the recipes were closely guarded family secrets. All I know is that the cheese had a unique orange look to it, and if you bit into a piece right out of the oven, the cheese would always stick to and burn the roof of your mouth.

The pizzas could be ordered plain, with pepperoni, or with any other toppings that you could find on a pizza. Probably, a high percentage of the pizzas ordered were either plain or pepperoni.

The final similarity between James' and Duke's was the fact that they were always crowded, and the only way you could get one of the best pizzas on earth was to call ahead and order or get there early enough. Both establishments made a limited amount of pizza dough, and when that was gone, they were out of pizzas for the evening. I'm not sure of the reasoning behind the rationing, but I can only figure that it had something to do with quality control. From a marketing point of view, it was also a smart move since you knew you had to beat the crowd in order to get served. I have to tell you, there was nothing more disappointing than getting dressed up and heading out with Mom and Dad with the idea of having pizza only to learn upon arriving that they had run out. Thankfully, we only lived a few blocks from James', and locals were always welcome!

Were there other pizza joints in town? You bet! And they were all good. It's just that I remember the triumvirate of Mr. Pizza, James', and Dukes as being the ones we most often visited.

Which was better? I'd really have to say it was a toss up between James' and Dukes, with James having the slight edge because you didn't have to drive clear up to the Heights to get a pizza— not that the drive wasn't worth it!

A true testament to the mouthwatering qualities of these three establishments is that they're all still open and cranking out pizzas in record numbers!

TELEVISION

The real difference between yesterday and today is that everything is done to excess these days. Take television, for example. Today you either have cable or a satellite dish, 500 plus channels, DVRs, DVDs, VCRs, TIVO, a box full of remotes, and a lot less time than you did decades ago to watch everything. Many people now spent more on cable/satellite television per month than my dad spent on his mortgage back in the sixties.

In the early sixties most of television was still black and white, and there were only a handful of shows on television. I grew up on a steady diet of "Leave it to Beaver," "The Munsters," and "The Andy Griffith Show."

Hanging out with my dad in our Shamokin Street living room—with our black and white television in the background!

Cartoons were a main reason for getting up early Saturday morning. Programmers knew that the best cartoons had to run early before kids headed outdoors to play. I can remember waking up at five o'clock on a Saturday morning, and cartoons were just starting. Several bowls of cereal and a few hours later, I had had enough of cartoons for the day. The sugar in cereal made me antsy enough that I felt the urge to get outside and run around just to burn it off!

Television spawned a lot of inventions—like the TV tray—a metal tray with folding legs that could be placed in front of an easy chair or couch in order to eat supper (or breakfast or lunch) while watching television. In fact, I think that it was television that broke up the family tradition of the family sitting around the supper table and conversing—you know, like the supper table scenes we would see on the shows we watched. Did you ever see the Beaver sitting in the living room with his mom and dad eating supper? Nope, not once, for every night June Cleaver had supper on the table and everyone sat around eating a balanced meal while finding out how school went (or what trouble the Beaver got into that day).

Another invention that caught on in a big way was the TV dinner. Imagine, a dinner, fast frozen and wrapped all in aluminum just waiting to be popped into the oven. Hey, the TV dinner was only a matter of time because you had to have something to put on the TV trays. Television was growing so popular in the sixties that if you had a new product, all you had to do was call it a TV something or other, and people would buy it. After all, attaching the moniker of TV in front of an item guaranteed that the family would use it while gathered in front of the television. Television had replaced the radio as the main source of information and entertainment.

One of the biggest gimmicks I had ever seen for television was a device that promised to turn your black and white television into a color set. Best of all, it was ninety-nine cents and could be purchased out of the back of any comic book! I remember our neighbors had one, and all of the kids gathered at our neighbors' house to watch a show in living color! I should explain that the device was nothing more than a large sheet of film—sort of what a large piece of x-ray film would look like—except that it was made up of bands of bright colors. The film stuck to your screen due to static electricity, and I'll never forget all of us sitting in front of the screen, marveling at the splash of colors that assaulted our eyes.

Sure, people were either red or blue or green, depending on their position on the screen, but nonetheless, we had indeed seen a show in color! I liken it to my first Atari™ game, Pong, and being mesmerized as a white square bounced across the television screen while two vertical lines served as paddles, whacking the "ball" back and forth. It was simple, but just like the color screen, we were growing up during the infancy of the electronic age. We eventually ended up with a color television set sometime, I believe, in the early seventies. Not a fake color set, but the real thing in living, breathing color.

After many years an interesting dilemma arose in my life with the explosion of cable networks. Today one of my favorite channels is TV Land, where I get to rekindle many of my childhood memories with reruns of classic television shows from the fifties, sixties, and seventies. One day something quite extraordinary happened; I actually saw an episode of "The Andy Griffith Show"—only it was in color! Befuddled, I stretched my imagination and couldn't ever recall seeing this show in color as a kid! The realization was that while we had a black and white television, a lot of my favorite shows were being broadcast in color. It amazes me whenever I see a favorite rerun of an old black and white show now being shown in color. It adds a whole new dimension to my viewing enjoyment.

PICNICS

Organized picnics in Shamokin were always special. It seemed that the entire town would turn out to partake of some of the best food you could ever imagine.

Typical family gatherings were all day affairs. Picnic baskets were packed with table cloths (usually red and white checkered) and all of the other trappings that went with the day—sandwiches, potato salad, and soda. Often the family picnic involved a day at the lake or at Knoebels under one of their covered pavilions. As a rule, covered pavilions were reserved for the ultimate family picnic—the family reunion. It wasn't unusual for a clan to get together annually down at Knoebels Grove and make a day of it. Some of the family reunions boasted an attendance of a hundred or more people—some folks driving in from several states away!

Picnics were such a common occurrence that a lot of the houses in Shamokin had their own picnic sheds—usually a metal covered roof in the back yard that had a set of picnic tables and a grill. No one really needed an excuse to have a picnic; it was just a great way to get out of the house and eat either prepared food or better yet, food cooked on a charcoal grill!

Organized church picnics were the really big shindigs, and it seemed that any occasion would be reason for a picnic. Of course, the church made tons of money from the picnics since most of the help and food was donated. Potato cakes, kielbasa, pierogies, hot dogs, hamburgers, and beer made up the biggest selling items at a church sponsored picnic. Often held at huge pavilions like the one

St. Stan's had near the cemetery, they could handle thousands of people who might turn out to partake. The really good picnics lasted two days, and tens of thousands of dollars could be raised.

If you haven't heard of these foods, I'll give you an overview of what you've been missing. Kielbasa was Polish sausage. Potato cakes were grated, seasoned potatoes that were fried on a hot skittle to a golden brown—and best eaten with a sprinkle of salt while being held in your hand. Pierogies were half-moon shaped pieces of dough that were stuffed with cheese, potato, cheese and potato, or cottage cheese. The pierogies were gently cooked in boiling water to make sure the dough was cooked through, and then also placed in a deep fryer and cooked to a golden brown. Also best sprinkled with salt, pierogies were sold by the thousands at an average picnic. An alternative to deep fried pierogies (and as far as I'm concerned the best way to eat them) was to take the pierogies out of the boiling water and to pan fry them swimming in butter and onions until lightly browned.

A rumor has it that there exists a variation to the pierogi—one stuffed with sauerkraut—that was popular with the Ukrainians. I can neither confirm nor deny this rumor since I've never tasted such a thing. But if you ever make it to Shamokin, check your calendar because chances are you can find an old-fashioned Polish picnic, complete with all the fixins'…and pierogies to die for!

KNOEBELS AMUSEMENT PARK

Close your eyes and imagine a place in a tranquil setting amongst mighty trees, complete with great food and all the fun of roller coaters, water slides, and other forms of entertainment that would entertain kids from eight to eighty. Now picture this place as having free parking and free admission.

If you've never lived in the Shamokin area, you may not be able to envision such a place. But if you grew up in central Pennsylvania, then you know that what I've just described really exists—it's Knoebels Amusement Park located just north of Elysburg.

I have no idea how this park arose, but I do know that it serves double duty as one of the best amusement parks hidden within a heavily forested section of the valley. Knoebels is owned by the Knoebels family, also known as one of the largest suppliers of lumber in the area. Picture an active lumber yard in the middle of the woods with an amusement park stuck in the middle. This scenic park is open from late spring to late fall, and it offers amusement for all ages. The beauty of the park is that there is no admission fee—and no parking fee. If you want to spend the day down at Knoebels and just people watch, all it will cost you is the gas in your car.

If you're a wooden rollercoaster fan, Knoebels has two of the largest active coasters in the United States—the world class Phoenix and the Twister. Ride that one only if you enjoy having your heart thrust up into your throat!

The Twister is over one hundred feet tall with the first vertical drop of eighty nine feet. A total length of thirty nine hundred feet, the Twister required over five hundred thousand board feet of lumber to complete!

Roller coasters are just a part of the fun at Knoebels. Miniature golf, bumper boats and cars, water slides, a haunted house, and dozens of other rides await park visitors willing to search out this extraordinary play place. Food also plays a big part in the park experience with a variety of options available; sit down restaurants and walk up vendors can be found scattered throughout the park. Then, of course, there are the aforementioned covered pavilions that can be reserved for picnics small and large. Reservations for pavilions are a must since many family reunions book their dates years in advance.

The author (foreground) enjoying one of the
many rides at Knoebels circa the early 1960s

Knoebels also has a large outdoor pool that fits in perfectly with the most demanding pool person. A small, narrow gauge train pulls happy parkgoers through the woods and past all the camp sites and cottages available for rent during the season.

While admission to the park is free, the food is available for purchase, and the rides are paid for on a ride-by-ride basis. Ticket booths sell books of tickets in various denominations so all of the kids can have a book of tickets to line up for their favorite rides.

I don't know when Knoebels first got its start as a park, but I do know that the same things we enjoyed there as kids were the very things that our parents enjoyed, too. In fact, parents were so comfortable with Knoebels that back in the late sixties and early seventies it wasn't an uncommon site for parents to drop off carloads of kids, reminding them to meet at the swimming pool when the park closed. Friday night in the summer usually meant a trip to Knoebels—and why not—it was hand stamp night! For a cheap one dollar and fifty cents, you could get your hand stamped and ride all of the rides for free, as many time as you wanted, from seven o'clock to closing at ten. We rode so many rides on a Friday night that I think it probably worked out to about a penny a ride!

Sadly, the one great staple of my childhood no longer exists at Knoebels—the roller skating rink. It seems kids just don't go for organized skating anymore, a real shame. The combination of colorful lights and snappy music made for harmless fun while getting a bit of exercise.

Speaking of exercise, one of the hardest rides at Knoebels was the cages. The cages were just that, giant cages that you were locked in to. It was made of wire mesh so you could see all around. The cage had handles inside, and you hung on to those as the attendant gave you a good hard push much like you would push someone starting out on a swing. Then you used your body weight and inertia to move the cage from side to side while gaining momentum. The idea was to go higher and higher each time until the cage would reach its peak, and then roll back down in a giant circle. The better you were at it, the more times you could make the cages go round and round. No longer available at Knoebels, the ride apparently fell victim to the times.

Besides the world class roller coaters at Knoebels, the real must-see attraction is the old fashion carousel. Hand-carved wooden horses, delicately painted, make up this beautiful carousel. The original music produced for this ride reminds you of the days when simple pleasures like this abounded.

While many of the simple pleasures I once enjoyed as a child ceased to exist years ago, it's nice to know that one last stronghold of old fashioned fun still stands tall among the trees—the amusement park known as Knoebels.

FUN SHOP

When was the last time you were in a store with a name that conveyed the store's very reason for being? Probably never! And yet there sits a store on Independence Street that is named the Fun Shop! And FUN is what it's all about!

The Fun Shop was and is a place to go to pick up the Sunday paper—just about any Sunday paper from anywhere! The papers were just the beginning of the treasures that could be found in the store. Housing one of the largest collections of greeting cards for every occasion, a person could spend all day reading the variety of cards.

Art supplies took up several rows of shelve space. Crayons, colored pencils, paints, framed canvasses, and construction paper in a rainbow of colors were just a few of the available art supplies. Colored paper streamers were also a big item, found in school colors of red for Lourdes High School and purple for Shamokin Area.

Also home to a variety of specialty items like pen and pencil sets, the Fun Shop provided me with endless hours of joy as I examined the inventory. Then there was always a friendly clerk who could answer any question I might have.

I also remember that the store was home to any type of Shamokin souvenir you could ever want: post cards of the Glen Burn culm bank, rock candy made to look like lumps of coal, statues carved out of coal—you name it, and you could find it at the Fun Shop. I don't know who the marketing genius was that came up with the name for the store, but I do know one thing for sure—every time I went into that corner shop, I had FUN!

FRIDAY NIGHT

A major transformation took place on downtown Independence Street on Friday nights. Shops closed, and the business people went home, as did the shoppers. A late night Friday on downtown Independence Street in the sixties and seventies meant one thing—teenagers—by the car loads!

Cruising Independence Street was a required rite of passage for the older kids in town. If you were old enough to drive, you had a car that you drove up one end of Independence Street and back down the other—over and over again. And why not—gas was thirty cents a gallon! If you weren't old enough to drive, you hoped you had a friend whose older brother would let you tag along.

If you didn't have a ride, you did the next best thing—you hung out on the street downtown in the hope that someone would pull up and offer a ride. Your odds of getting a ride depended on whether you were one of the girls or one of the guys.

Hot cars abounded up and down the street—the louder the better! Mustangs were all the rage back before they were considered classics, and Barracudas and Novas cruised the strip on a Friday night. Seeing just how many kids could pile into one car was also a favorite pastime. Driving the strip was usually harmless fun, reminiscent of a scene right out of George Lucas' *American Graffiti*.

If the kids weren't cruising the streets of downtown, they were hanging out at their version of Al's diner—Spangenberg's Tast-T-Freez. Home to a variety of tasty delights—but mostly ice cream—Spangenberg's was the place to park and enjoy a cool treat with your friends! Located just down Route 61, it consisted of a single, stand alone building with a large parking lot. Soft serve ice cream was a real treat with some of the best sundaes this side of Martz's Ice Cream Parlor! Spangenberg's special was the Big T burger—double patties with pickle, onion, mustard and special sauce that made their hamburgers taste unique. Golden brown fries topped off the meal, all of which you ate from the comfort of your car. If you were one of the cool kids, you got to spend time at Spangenberg's in a convertible with the top down! Everyone played the local radio station on their car radios (we only had one local station back then), but there really wasn't a need because Spangenberg's had these huge stadium-like speakers on the corners of the building that always belted out the tunes that kids enjoyed hearing.

The author outside of present-day Spangenberg's
ordering a tasty treat!

Another advantage of Spangenberg's was going up to the order widow and placing an order. As I recall, Spangey's (what the cool kids called it) always hired the best looking girls to work the front order windows. Not only was there great food to be had, but there was nothing better than looking through the glass windows and seeing a good looking girl preparing it for you. As I recall, they all had to wear uniforms that were white dresses. Given the styles of the day usually meant short hemlines on the dresses, and the really good looking girls also wore white stockings. There was nothing better than watching one of Spangey's girls squirting whipped cream on the top of your sundae!

CEREAL SATURDAY

When we were kids, we ate more cereal than any previous generation. Was it that cereal was so good we couldn't live without it? Probably not, since most cereal was sugar disguised as something else. I guess adults figured as long as we were putting cereal in our milk, it was probably good for us.

There was a deep, dark cereal secret amongst kids that was sort of an unwritten rule—don't ever, ever let Mom go shopping for cereal without you. Letting Mom pick out the cereal was like letting kids pick out what car Dad should buy! The secret was to convince her that you should pick out the cereal while at the grocery store. Often, just promising that you would eat all the cereal was enough to seal the deal.

As you've probably figured out, kids never bought cereal for how good it tasted because it all tasted pretty much the same. How different can you make pure sugar taste? Sure, you can disguise it with marshmallows and chocolate, but all you're really doing is adding more sugar! The key to cereal-buying was searching out the coolest free prize included in the box! For my money (well, Mom's money) Cap'n Crunch™ seemed to have the best prizes. As an added incentive, most of the cereal boxes had games and/or puzzles on the back of the boxes. A really cool box was one that had cut out cardboard figures that you could clip and play with.

One of my favorite toys was the plastic submarine that you could put in the tub. First, you had to fill it with baking soda. Then the sub would sink and resurface as the baking soda became wet (or maybe it was the other way around—who can understand such complex things when you're eight years old?)

One of the golden rules of cereal eating was that it was only to be eaten at breakfast time. The free prizes were always in the very bottom of the cereal package. The less imaginative kids would actually eat all of the cereal before getting to the prize, but some of us designed a few simple tactics to get to the toy without having to eat any of the cereal.

The first ploy was the simplest—open the box, tear open the inner package, and bury your hand clear up to your elbow, digging to the bottom for the toy. Hey, it was your arm, and you were the only one going to eat the cereal, so who really cared?

Most of the other tricks only worked when Mom and Dad were still in bed—which is why I figured cartoons were on so early in the morning on Saturdays. It was a ploy by the cereal companies and cartoon makers to sell more cereal. Another trick that usually backfired was opening the box from the bottom, enabling you to get to the bottom of the cereal first. Of course putting the box of cereal back on the shelf usually meant forgetting about the opened box and having the bottom fall out, spilling cereal all over the floor.

The other option, my favorite, was taking one of Mom's big mixing bowls and pouring the contents of the entire box into the bowl—it was fast and simple, and the toy inside always ended up on the top of the stack. It was a simple matter to pour the cereal back into the box, leaving the appearance that the toy was still safely on the bottom of the bag.

The final option was to eat so much cereal, usually three or four bowls at a time, that you worked your way to the prize. Now eating three or four bowls of cereal with milk while watching cartoons on a Saturday morning was the equivalent of lighting the fuse on a powder keg and then sitting on it, waiting for it to go off! Thankfully, that was one of the purposes of owning a dog. On any given Saturday, unbeknownst to my parents, I fed as much cereal to the dog as I ate!

Today's cereal shelves contain a multitude more of choices, but most of the offers are redemptions requiring a kid to save so many box tops or go online to enter a code or some other gimmick.

What cereal manufacturers of today fail to recognize is that when you're eight years old and want something, you want it right away! Of course, the one thing they haven't forgotten is to how to spin pure sugar into something that a kid will crave while packaging it appealingly enough for a parent to want to buy it!

GRADUATION

Graduating from anything is a glorious occasion marking a milestone or great achievement. Not so graduating from St. Stan's back in 1971! Sure, it was nice to make it past the eighth grade, but we were about to give up our status as eight graders to become lowly freshmen in high school. We all know what happens to freshmen in high school—not a pretty sight. Believe me, I know because when I was in eighth grade, we all treated the fifth, sixth, and seventh graders the same way. Knowing how terrible we were to the younger kids only fueled the fires of expectation of what we were going to face in high school—and we had the entire summer to worry about it!

Compounding the problem was the fact that many of us had to make a momentous decision—go to school at Our Lady of Lourdes High School with four more years of nuns, religion, and uniforms or head out for the hallowed halls of Shamokin Area High School. Both schools had their pluses and minuses, and I, at least, had the chance to make up my own mind.

Typically, graduation from parochial school meant four more years of the same, except for the fact that it wasn't the way it was done when our parents went to school. Back in my parents' time, the Shamokin area didn't have a Catholic high school, so the prescribed course was eight years of Catholic school followed up with four more years of public school.

Conventional wisdom was that you tended to get a better education from parochial school. I'm here to debunk that belief right now! Don't misunderstand me. We got a great education at St. Stan's, where we learned a lot of the basics that we needed to get by in the world. We also learned a deep rooted respect for our peers. But the curriculum didn't even come close to matching that of the local public schools. Not that the curriculum in public school was better—it was just a lot different.

The thought of normal people teaching me, no more nuns, was something that appealed to me, so I signed up to attend the local public school—a decision that my parents let me make for myself. If

Graduation day procession from St. Stan's School—May 1971

there was any redeeming value to attending public school, it was that while we entered as freshmen, we weren't just thrust into the high school environment. Instead, we went to middle school, which was the public school equivalent of a buffer between elementary school and high school.

I entered middle school in the ninth grade and was once again at the high end of the pecking order. Unfortunately, just about all of my classmates went on to Catholic high school, so I was left to fend for myself without any friends to back me up. It was about a week

103

into the new school year before I got beat up by a kid who didn't even go to our school.

Ninth grade for me was bittersweet! School was harder than at St. Stan's by default since my education didn't match the public school curriculum. Taking Spanish, algebra (or was it trigonometry) and earth and space science was almost more than I could handle.

Another nightmare was gym class—once a week. When we went to St. Stan's, we didn't have gym class. Gym was considered a waste of time. If a kid didn't get enough exercise just being a kid, it was his own fault. As horrible as gym class was (climbing up a knotted rope twenty feet off the floor?), it was *after* gym class that sent shivers up my spine. Our gym coach was this short, stocky ex-marine (weren't they all?), and he insisted that everyone had to take a shower before leaving the gym. I know the anxiety of taking a shower after gym class is a stereotype scenario in every teen flick made in the past fifty years, but it was a real fear. I had never seen another guy naked in my entire life, and having to see a room full of prepubescent kids all taking a shower at the same time in those open, shared showers was enough to make me throw up. I can only imagine how the kids that hadn't yet developed pubic hair felt!

The first week of public school for me was a real eye-opener. The halls of St. Stan's were sterile by comparison, as there was a real sameness to everyone thanks to the uniforms we had to wear. Not public school—kids dressed the way they wanted, and the girls especially looked different as they wore more form fitting clothes that showed off their developing bodies. In my first week of school I had seen boys and girls holding hands, kissing—KISSING—passing cigarettes, joints, and heard curse words that I had never heard before!

I eventually got past those negative experiences and the feelings they generated as I worked hard at trying to fit in. Thanks to some of the more popular girls in ninth grade who befriended me like a person would a lost puppy, I was able to endure what was otherwise a pretty miserable four years of high school!

ABOUT THE COVER

The Ragamuffins of the Fifth Ward cover was designed by the author to capture the essence of growing up in a small coal mining town in central Pennsylvania. The kids sitting curbside perfectly captured the mood of those bygone days of the 1960s. Comics, trading cards, and candy—along with pick-up baseball games—were a daily ritual in similar small communities throughout the country. The background displays the familiar row house architecture found in the northeast. As a point of reference, the row houses as represented in the artwork are the artist's rendering based on a photograph provided by the author. The photo was undated and depicts the author's grandmother's house located on Pearl Street in Shamokin.

ABOUT THE ARTISTS

Claude St. Aubin is a Canadian-based artist who has worked on a variety of comic books. Claude St. Aubin and Charles Novinskie first worked together on licensed properties during Novinskie's tenure as editor and sales and promotions manager for Topps Comics. Claude has drawn a variety of licensed characters based on properties ranging from Jurassic Park, James Bond, and Zorro. Claude modeled the penciled cover art for *Ragamuffins of the Fifth Ward* upon an idea provided by the author.

Jaysin Brunner is a talented computer colorist/painter. Living in Calgary, Alberta, Jaysin has provide color artwork for a variety of comic books and magazines. Taking the finished black and white artwork for *Ragamuffins of the Fifth Ward*, Jaysin transformed the work into a full-color representation of life in the sixties.

The real Ragamuffins of the Fifth Ward circa 1963

Thanks for the memories—without all of you
this book would never have been possible!

Fine Publications from Edit et Cetera Ltd.
Visit our website: www.family bookhouse.com

KATHERINE'S SONG by Linda Lane. (Nov. 2003) Katherine Kohler has it all…a loving husband, a wonderful family, a great job…everything she ever wanted. But it ends when her dear Edmund dies tragically, leaving her the family business. Now she must honor a promise that takes her in a direction she never wanted to go.

She reels with pain when her younger daughter blames her for Ed's death. Then she learns that, on the last day he lived, her husband made an offer to her despised brother-in-law. And *she's* expected to fulfill it.

Oren Kohler looks enough like his deceased brother to be his twin, but there the similarity ends. A manipulative opportunist with a diabolical mind, a chip on his shoulder, and a vendetta against women, he has come to settle an old score with his sister-in-law.

The secret Oren has kept from all of them adds another ingredient to the mix that threatens to destroy everything that was dear to his brother. Will Katherine overcome her grief in time to mend her relationship with her daughter, save the family business, and reach our for a new life of her own?

A must-read for lovers of compelling stories and family fiction.

GRAND RIVER STUDENT ANTHOLOGY 2004 (May 2004) Working in conjunction with Mesa State College professor, poet, and owner of Farolito Press, Dr. L. Luis Lopez, and Marco Weber of Readmoor Books, Edit et Cetera Ltd. published the works of some 200 students in the Grand Valley, a region that includes Grand Junction, Colorado, and surrounding areas.

Inundated with several hundred entries from hopeful students, grades K-12, we were assisted with the difficult process of choosing those papers that would become part of this pilot project by a panel of Mesa State honors students. Even our cover was designed by a seventh-grader. After publication, we held a full day of readings, during which time more than half of those published read their works in front of family and friends who came to applaud their efforts.

The students who submitted entries touched our hearts with their insight, their honesty, their hopes, their pain, their dreams, and their writing ability. We salute them! At Edit et Cetera Ltd. we encourage reading at all ages and advocate the advancement of literacy worldwide.

PAPILLONS by Clementine de Blanzat. (Mar. 2004) This exquisite book of poems, written originally in French and presented here with accompanying English renditions, opens up a new world to all, even those who typically do not read poetry. The honest feelings that leap from its pages express realities that are a part of all of us.

Not only do Ms. de Blanzat's words touch the heart, but also they speak to the soul, the very depths of who we are and who we want to be. From the whimsical "Leap-Frog" to the poignant "If I Were You..." to the pain of "His Land," the reader is wrapped in the web of emotions that this talented poet so eloquently has spun.

This unique book of poems belongs on the bedside table of all who long to touch and experience the realities of love, of pain, of hope, of life. An incredible expression of the heart, "Papillons" will draw the reader again and again to its wonderful pages.

FRUITS OF THE FAMINE by L. Katherine Dailey. (Oct. 2004) Driven from her home after her father dies, Amanda Darby leaves her native Ireland and sails to America under an assumed name. She doesn't expect to fall in love—nor does she expect to be the subject of a criminal investigation—but life is full of the unexpected.

Afraid to tell her wealthy suitor her awful secret, she learns by accident that he has one of his own, one that can destroy any chance they have for happiness. And just in case it doesn't, his scheming brother will.

This beautifully written coming-of-age novel begins during the Irish famine that destroyed or dislocated one-quarter of the population between 1845 and 1851, and continues in 1875, when the daughter of a famine survivor seeks to make sense of the devastating tragedy that forever altered their lives.

Fine Publications from Stepping Stones Press Ltd.
Visit our website: www.steppingstonespress.com

DAY OF RETRIBUTION by Tom Trench. (Oct. 2004) This thriller focuses on the lives of three executives entangled in a life-threatening crisis. David Coleman is caught between a boss who didn't want to hire him and an employee who has been on the take for years—right under his nose. Landon Walters would like nothing better than to see David on his way down the road and his close friend, Alex Carter, in his place. Alex, a master of deception who struggles daily to control his unrelenting anger, views David 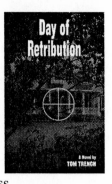 as the sole obstacle standing in the way of his success.

One man will survive with his job in tact. Another will lose both face and position. And still another will not survive at all.

Day of Retribution explores the rewards of success as well as the devastation of failed ambitions within the framework of a tough, profit-driven corporation. It also addresses the impact of childhood abuse on the life of the adult victim. This story is told with passion, honesty, and sensitivity.

LOOKING FOR OUR PUBLICATIONS?

- Visit our website at www.familybookhouse.com
- Ask your favorite bookstore to order our books. They are distributed through Ingram's and Baker and Taylor and are available to bookstores from these sources.
- Check your local library. If you don't see our books on the shelf, ask the librarian to order them.
- Our publications are also available at www.amazon.com and www.bn.com. You can search by title or by author.

Printed in the United States
33372LVS00002B/106-111